THE GAMES AND THE PLAYERS YOU'LL NEVER FORGET!

They're the longshots who beat the odds, the underdog teams who creamed the favorites, the aging fighters who came back for one more bout and made history. Meet the Cinderella teams and players who made miracles: the 1980 U.S. Olympic Hockey Team; the Washington Redskins in the 1988 Super Bowl; the 1985 World Series' Kansas City Royals and the 1987 Minnesota Twins, each battling the favored St. Louis Cardinals; the Portland Trailblazers in the 1977 NBA Playoffs; Joe Namath's New York Jets in the greatest upset in the history of NFL football—the 1968 championships; Muhammad Ali in the 1974 world heavyweight title bout, and Sugar Ray Leonard fighting for the middleweight title in 1987; Villanova's surprise upset over champion Georgetown in 1985 to win the NCAA basketball title; and the magic Mets of 1969. . . .

It's all in the game—and all the games are here, in the book that's every sports fan's dream!

Books by Bill Gutman

Sports Illustrated/BASEBALL'S RECORD BREAKERS
Sports Illustrated/GREAT MOMENTS IN BASEBALL
Sports Illustrated/GREAT MOMENTS IN PRO FOOTBALL
Sports Illustrated/PRO FOOTBALL'S RECORD BREAKERS
Sports Illustrated/STRANGE AND AMAZING BASEBALL
  STORIES
Sports Illustrated/STRANGE AND AMAZING FOOTBALL
  STORIES
BASEBALL'S HOT NEW STARS
GREAT SPORTS UPSETS
STRANGE AND AMAZING WRESTLING STORIES

Available from ARCHWAY Paperbacks

GREAT SPORTS UPSETS

BILL GUTMAN

AN ARCHWAY PAPERBACK
Published by POCKET BOOKS

New York   London   Toronto   Sydney   Tokyo   Singapore

Cover photos (clockwise from top right): Sugar Ray Leonard and Marvin Hagler, Bill Walton, Patrick Ewing, Tom Seaver, Joe Namath, and the 1980 U.S. Olympic hockey victory

AN ARCHWAY PAPERBACK *Original*

An Archway Paperback published by
POCKET BOOKS, a division of Simon & Schuster
1230 Avenue of the Americas, New York, NY 10020

Copyright © 1988 by Bill Gutman
Cover photo copyright © 1988 Focus on Sports Inc.

ISBN: 0-671-70925-9

First Archway Paperback printing November 1988

10 9 8 7 6 5 4

AN ARCHWAY PAPERBACK and colophon are
registered trademarks of Simon & Schuster.

Printed in the U.S.A.

IL 5+

Contents

Introduction

Everyone loves an underdog. That's been an American sports axiom for a long time. Fans love to root for the individual or team that isn't supposed to win, the perennial loser that has suddenly come alive.

Great Sports Upsets tells the stories of teams and individuals who weren't supposed to win but, through grit and determination, and great athletic talent, have emerged victorious. Whether it be on the diamond, the gridiron, the hardwood, the ice, or in the boxing ring, these greats upsets have captured the imagination of fans everywhere.

The 1980 United States Olympic ice hockey team helped draw a nation together when it upset the mighty Russian team for the gold medal. The 1987 Minnesota Twins showed how a Cinderella team could win the World Series. Sugar Ray Leonard upset everyone's predictions when he shook off five years of ring rust to defeat middleweight champion Marvelous Marvin Hagler.

These are just some of the stories chronicled in *Great Sports Upsets*. Along with them are the exploits of such legendary athletes as Joe Namath, Muhammad Ali, Bill Walton, and Tom Seaver. At one time or another all were underdogs and part of a great upset. Their stories, too, help make the following pages jump to life with nonstop sports action.

The One-Quarter Upset

There are those who'll argue that the the 1988 Super Bowl was not an upset. They'll say it was a toss-up, almost a pick-em game. Both teams, the Washington Redskins and Denver Broncos, had assets and liabilities, and the actual flow of the game would determine the eventual winner.

Well, it flowed, all right. Oh, boy, did it flow. In fact, it flowed one way, then the other. And when it flowed the other way in the second period, there was an avalanche of offensive football the likes of which was rarely seen on a professional football field, and never seen in a game the magnitude of the Super Bowl.

The offensive explosion defied expectation and convention, and what's more, the quarterback who was supposed to be capable of attaining those heights wasn't the one who scaled them. It was the other guy, the guy who wasn't even supposed to be there in the first place. And that's why it was an upset. It upset all logic and rationale on the gridiron.

Until the Super Bowl, the 1987 football season was best remembered as the year of the strike. NFL players went out for some five weeks. One game was wiped completely from the schedule, four others were played with replacement players, more commonly known as "scabs." It's said that scab football effectively ruined the season. Some teams, like the defending Super Bowl champion New York Giants, had a scab team that lost all four of its games. As a result, the Giants didn't even make it to the playoffs a year after winning it all.

But some teams continued to thrive. One of them was the Washington Redskins. Long considered one of the best organized and best coached teams in the NFL, the Skins have prospered under general manager Bobby Beathard and head coach Joe Gibbs. They had a fine team to begin with, but even their scab team was good, and continued winning while the regulars were on strike.

As a result, the Skins won the NFC Eastern Division title, replacing the Giants in the top spot. But they weren't a lock to make the Super Bowl, since the NFC had two other teams considered among the best in the league, the Chicago Bears and San Francisco 49ers. In fact, many considered the Niners the class of the entire NFL in 1987.

If the Skins had one possible key weakness, it was at the quarterback position. Young Jay Schroeder, only in his second full season, was the starter at the outset and coming off a fine 1986 campaign. He was widely touted as a coming star of the league. But Schroeder stumbled at the beginning of the season, and still looked shaky when he returned after the strike. More and more Redskin fans began looking at the backup quarterback, wondering how he'd fare with the number-one job.

The backup was a nine-year veteran in his first year with the Redskins. His name was Doug Williams, a strong-armed QB who had gone to Grambling College and was one of the first starting quarterbacks in the NFL who happened also to be a black man.

Williams had started his pro career with the expansionist Tampa Bay Buccaneers and learned his trade the hard way, often running for his life and taking innumerable hard licks from defensive linemen and linebackers. Though he had passed the Bucs into the playoffs a couple of times, he was never really considered among the top signalcallers in the league. Finally, Williams jumped to the new United States Football League, where he hoped to find a friendlier home away from the boos and catcalls that Tampa Bay fans reserved for him whenever the team faltered.

With the USFL gone, Williams returned to Washington and the NFL, hoping to get one more chance to grab the brass ring, and establish himself as a bona fide starting quarterback in the NFL. At the outset of the season he was content to play behind Schroeder and wait his turn. And when he finally got it, midway through the season, he played well, so well in fact, that it began to look as if the job was his. Then he sustained a neck injury that put him on the shelf for a few games.

3

Doug Williams started the year as the Redskins'
backup quarterback, only to become the Most Valuable Player in the 1988 Super Bowl with a record-
breaking performance. (Courtesy Washington Redskins)

"I finally get a chance and this happens," he lamented as Schroeder reclaimed the starting job. "I guess I'll have to wait again."

But when the Skins won the NFC East and got ready for the playoffs, Coach Gibbs named Doug Williams his starting quarterback once more. And Williams responded, playing brilliantly as the Redskins defeated the always-tough Chicago Bears to advance to the NFC title game against the Minnesota Vikings, who were playing the Cinderella role. The Vikes had upset the mighty San Francisco 49ers in an explosive display of offensive football. The Redskins were favored, but many people were picking upset.

Meanwhile in the AFC, the Denver Broncos were on a course they hoped would put them in a second straight Super Bowl. A year earlier the Broncs had reached the super game only to be derailed by the New York Giants, 39–20. So the Broncos felt they had something to prove.

In Denver, there was no quarterback controversy. The Broncos were led by John Elway, a strong-armed thrower and rugged runner who was one of the best in the game. Elway had come out of Stanford University with a rifle of an arm and the ability to make the big play. It took him a couple of years to adjust to the pro game, but many now considered him the most dangerous and dominant quarterback in football. He had tremendous athletic ability, could scramble and throw on the run as well as anyone.

Elway had really come to national prominence in the AFC title game a year earlier. The Broncos were trail-

5

ing the Cleveland Browns by seven points with only minutes left when Elway engineered a brilliant, 98-yard touchdown drive to tie the game. He then led his club to a victory in overtime and a trip to the Super Bowl.

As is often the case in conference title games and in the Super Bowl, the quarterbacks become the center of attention. Sometimes another player can rise up to capture the spotlight, but somehow the games always seem to revolve around the QB.

In the NFC title game, the Redskins had to pull out all the stops to beat the Vikings, 17–10. Minnesota proved a formidable foe, and the game was even tougher because quarterback Williams had a miserable game. He completed just 9 of 26 passes for 119 yards. And while he threw for a pair of scores, he also heard plenty of boos from the sellout crowd at Robert F. Kennedy Stadium in Washington.

The Skins first score came on a 98-yard drive that featured a 28-yard end around by receiver Ricky Sanders, and a 42-yard touchdown pass from Williams to running back Kelvin Bryant. But after that score, Williams began missing on his passes, and late in the second quarter the Vikings were able to tie the game at 7–7. It stayed that way at the half, and while some of the fans were yelling for Schroeder, Coach Gibbs had no intention of changing quarterbacks.

"Doug knew what he was doing," the coach said. "He never lost his poise. When he had to throw the ball away, he did it. It might have looked bad in the stands, but there was a reason. When a quarterback comes off the field, you look at his eyes, and sometimes see indecision or confusion. There was never anything I saw in Doug's eyes that made me worry."

Early in the fourth quarter the game was still tied at 10–10 as the two teams exchanged field goals. But then the Redskins came back to march 70 yards for the go-ahead score. Williams hit Gary Clark with a short pass that turned into a 43-yard gain, then hit Clark again from seven yards out for the TD. The kick made it 17–10.

Minnesota had one last chance, driving from their own 33 to the Washington 6-yard line, where they had a second-and-four with 1:05 left. Two incompletions left them with a fourth-down play that could mean the ballgame. Quarterback Wade Wilson dropped back and threw for running back Darrin Nelson at the goal line.

Nelson lunged for the ball, got his hands on it . . . and dropped it! Washington just had to run out the clock to win. They were on their way to the Super Bowl.

In the AFC title game, Denver and Cleveland had a rematch of their classic from the year before, and this one turned out to be every bit as exciting. John Elway was nearly the whole show in the first half, directing the Broncos to a commanding, 21–3 lead.

But in the second half, Browns' quarterback Bernie Kosar led his team to touchdowns on their first four possessions. Suddenly, Elway was playing catch-up. He connected with receiver Mark Jackson for an 80-yard, pass-run touchdown, and with just 5:14 left, led his club on a 75-yard drive that again gave them the lead at 38–31. On that drive, Elway connected twice with Ricky Nattiel for 52 yards, then lobbed a perfect pass to running back Sammy Winder for a 20-yard score.

With the score 38–31, Cleveland then made a last-ditch drive. Kosar had his club at the Denver eight. He gave the ball to running back Ernest Byner, who sprinted around the left side and appeared to be heading in for the tying touchdown. Only Jeremiah Castille stripped Byner of the ball at the one and recovered it at the three. The game was saved and Denver was headed for a return trip to the Super Bowl.

In the two weeks preceding the big game, there was the usual bombardment of Super Bowl hype. Every aspect of the game was analyzed, dissected, broken down, diagnosed, and speculated upon. But in the minds of many, the difference was going to be the superior ability of John Elway compared to the average ability of Doug Williams. And Williams seemed to be hearing more questions about his being the first black quarterback to start a Super Bowl game than about the game itself.

But the 32-year-old journeyman kept his cool and answered all the questions, no matter how many times they were asked.

"Joe Gibbs and Bobby Beathard didn't bring me in to be the first black quarterback in the Super Bowl," he said. "They brought me in to be the quarterback of the Washington Redskins."

Williams also said he preferred to be thought of as a role model for all young players, white and black alike, though he admitted he was glad if he had opened doors

8

for other young black quarterbacks coming into the NFL. He also said he didn't feel that he was the only key to a Washington win.

"I don't have to play well for us to win," he said. "What I have to do is not beat the Redskins by throwing interceptions or turning the ball over."

Still, the pregame hype focused on the Washington defense and the job it would have stopping John Elway. Most analysts viewed this as the biggest key to the game. And the way things started at San Diego's Jack Murphy Stadium, it looked as if the analysts were right.

The first time Elway touched the football he made the analysts look like geniuses. With the ball at the Denver 44, he took the snap, dropped back, and fired down the right side. There was receiver Ricky Nattiel, beating cornerback Barry Wilburn and grabbing the perfect pass to complete a 56-yard touchdown play. The huge crowd was shocked as Rich Karlis booted the extra point to make it a 7–0 game.

Washington couldn't go and Denver got the ball back at its own 32. Once again Elway moved his club effortlessly, this time bringing them all the way to the Washington seven before the drive stalled. Karlis finally came on and kicked a field goal from the 24, giving the Broncos a 10–0 lead still early in the first quarter. Elway was living up to all his advance notices.

Williams, meanwhile, seemed to be struggling. He didn't appear to have his rhythm or his confidence and just wasn't looking sharp. It was still a 10–0 game late in the opening quarter when the Redskin quarterback dropped back to pass. Suddenly, his right leg slid out from under him and he went down, a look of extreme pain on his face. He had twisted his left knee.

He got up and tried to walk back to the huddle. But the knee just went out and he was down. On the sidelines, Schroeder began to warm up quickly. Sure enough, Williams had to leave the game. The question was the seriousness of the injury and whether or not he would return.

Schroeder didn't look much better in the short time he was in there. He was sacked once and threw an incompletion. But when the Skins got the ball back again, Doug Williams was once again at the helm, his knee wrapped, but apparently sound. And during this time, Elway had stopped moving his team. In fact, after his blistering start, his game suddenly seemed off. His passes were no longer on the mark and in some ways he appeared to be forcing the ball.

When the second quarter began, Denver had the ball and had moved to the Washington 36 with a third-and-five play coming up. But Elway's pass was dropped, and following a kick, Washington wound up with the ball at their own 20. Williams dropped back and looked for speedy Ricky Sanders, who was streaking downfield past cornerback Mark Haynes. The quarterback let the ball fly and Sanders took it in full stride, racing all the way to the end zone for an 80-yard score.

The kick made it 10–7 and suddenly the Redskins were back in it. This was usually when Elway would come right back. But this time the Broncos couldn't move the ball and their quarterback threw his fifth and

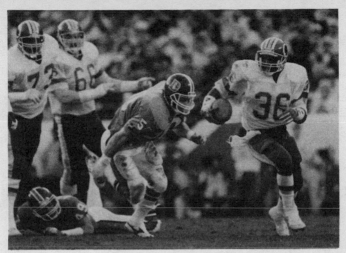

Rookie running back Timmy Smith (36) was not only a surprise starter in Super Bowl XXII, but wound up rushing for more than 200 yards in yet another record-breaking performance in the Redskins' upset of the Denver Broncos. (AP/Wide World Photo)

six consecutive incompletions. He wasn't hitting. What would Williams now do for an encore?

With the ball at the 36, the Skins began driving. Mixing his plays, Williams was suddenly looking like a confident quarterback. He was utilizing a rookie tailback, Timmy Smith, who was a surprise starter in place of veteran George Rogers, and Smith was producing. The quick rookie ran for 19 yards on one play to keep the drive going. Finally, with the ball at the Denver 27, Williams tossed a scoring pass to wide receiver Gary Clark. The kick made it a 14–10 game, and the Skins had scored on two straight possessions.

Once again Elway tried to rally his team. He managed to get the Broncos all the way to the Washington 26. But the Redskin defense toughened again and then Karlis missed on a 43-yard field-goal try. So Washington had the ball for the third time in the quarter.

Williams went to work once more. He hit Clark for 16 yards, bringing the ball to the 48. Then he gave it to rookie Smith again. This time the young fullback tried the right side on a counter-gap play. Following his blocks, he burst through the line, used a few of his own moves, and was suddenly in the clear and on his way to an electrifying, 58-yard touchdown run. It was the Skins' third TD of the period and they now had a 21–10 lead.

Minutes later Washington had the ball again and promptly went 60 yards on just two plays. The first was a 10-yard toss to Sanders, followed immediately by another bomb to the former USFL star, this one covering 50 yards. The kick made it a 28–10 game, with the Skins very much in command.

But they weren't through yet. Elway went deep looking for Nattiel, but the ball was picked off by Wilburn, and the Redskins got it on their 21. Williams went right back to Smith, who used the same play he had run for a score, but this time to the left side. It worked once more, and Smith sped for 43 yards before being hit.

As Washington guard R. C. Thielemann put it, "They [the Broncos] were in shock. They couldn't believe we were running for this kind of yardage on them."

Before the half ended, the Skins drove one more time, with Williams throwing his fourth scoring pass of the period, an eight-yarder to tight end Clint Didier. The fans in San Diego were in shock. The quarter had started with Denver in the lead at 10–0. Less then 15 minutes later, Washington had an incredible, 35–10 advantage. And it took a record-setting performance, led by the "other" quarterback in the game, to do it.

In setting a postseason record of five touchdowns in a period, the Skins had also compiled an incredible 356 yards in total offense. Williams was 9 for 11 in the period, good for 228 yards and four touchdowns. It was a single-quarter blitzkrieg the likes of which had never been seen before. And it all but destroyed the Broncos.

They could never get going again, and Washington coasted home for one of the easiest Super Bowl wins ever, 42–10. Williams, who was named the Most Valuable Player, completed 18 passes in 29 tries for a record 340 yards and four scores. Ricky Sanders also set a Super Bowl mark with 193 receiving yards, while Timmy Smith set a new rushing standard with 204 yards on 22 carries.

As a team, the Skins went into the record books with 602 total yards, 280 of which came on the ground. But it was that wild second quarter that won the game, that upset all the pregame predictions.

As for John Elway, who was supposed to dominate the game—well, he just didn't have it. He was only 14 for 38 in the passing department for 257 yards and one score. He had three tosses intercepted, seven deflected, and he was sacked by the aggressive Redskin defense five times. And at the end, the emotions of the two quarterbacks were poles apart.

Said Elway, "I know a lot of quarterbacks never reach the Super Bowl. But as far as I'm concerned, my ultimate goal is to win this game. I won't have a good feeling about myself until I win one."

On the other side of the fence, someone asked Doug Williams if he could express the joy he felt at winning and being the MVP.

"Not yet," he said happily, still letting the events of the day sink in. "Catch me next week back home in Louisiana."

Unlikely heroes, unlikely moments. Upsets will do that for you.

Miracle on Ice

Back in 1960, the United States ice hockey team won an Olympic Gold Medal. It was a considerable achievement then, as the Americans came to Squaw Valley, California, and conquered all the other countries on the ice. But after that, most observers of the ice sport wondered if it could ever happen again.

For after the 1960 games, the Soviet Union began building an amateur hockey program that would soon become the best in the world. In the following four Winter Olympic Games (1964, '68, '72, and '76), the Russian skaters dominated the ice, taking the gold medal each time.

And during this period the United States program seemed to weaken. The best amateur players were getting into the professional National Hockey League as quickly as the big dollars beckoned, and not all the others wanted the grind of getting ready for the Olympics, where the Russians, the Canadians, the Czechs, and the Swedes usually awaited with fine teams.

With the Winter Olympics returning to the United States and Lake Placid, New York, in 1980, the U.S. Olympic Committee was hoping to put a representative team on the ice, a team that might have at least an outside shot at a medal. The Russians, of course, would once again be heavy favorites to take the gold. As usual, they would have a veteran team, one that was adept at skating and passing as it was with the more physical checking game.

Herb Brooks, who had coached the University of Minnesota hockey team to several national championships, was chosen to coach the Olympians. A no-nonsense guy and longtime admirer of the slick European style of hockey, Brooks took the job with just one goal in mind—to win. And he went about putting together the best aggregate squad he could find.

There was a long tryout period in which Brooks slowly weeded out the players he didn't want, while trying to choose the final squad in a way that would result in the most balanced team, a team that could skate with the others, but also bump with them if necessary.

While many of Brooks's players were from the Midwest, players with whom he was already familiar through college competition, two of his most important additions were from the Boston area. Forward Mike Eruzione, a 25-year-old from Boston University, who was never good enough for the NHL, became the team's captain; and Jim Craig, who had led Boston University to the collegiate championship in 1978, was the goaltender.

The team was formed in August, and for the next six months prior to the start of the games in February, they worked together, playing a grueling, 62-game schedule marked by frequent ups and downs, and some conflicts between the players and their unsmiling, hard-driving coach. Then, on the eve of the Olympics, the United States team played an exhibition game against the Russian team at Madison Square Garden in New York City.

It resulted in a disastrous, 10–3 defeat for the Americans, once again dimming any hopes they might have harbored for a gold medal. And it pointed out, all over again, just how powerful the Russian hockey program was. The Soviets had already showed they were good enough to beat National Hockey League teams, so how could this team of young American players hope to beat them? It would take a miracle, many people thought.

There were some experts, of course, who thought it was possible. Bill Torrey, the general manager of the NHL New York Islanders, put it this way.

"For the first time," Torrey said, "a Western team prepared properly for the Soviets. And when you've got that type of preparation, and then add to that the emotion of a short tournament, a playoff-type series, the U.S. put itself in a great position to do very well in Lake Placid."

Even the players themselves didn't know quite what

to expect. High-scoring forward Mark Johnson, who was an all-American at the University of Wisconsin and college hockey's Player of the Year in 1979, said the players came to Lake Placid wondering just what would happen.

"When we first arrived, we weren't quite sure how we stacked up against all the European teams," Johnson said. "I mean, coming off the Garden loss, the Russians, and the 62-game exhibition schedule, we were kind of wondering just where we stood."

Coming in, the 20 players on the United States team were joined in a single cause. They had been together for a full six months and had played the equivalent of nearly a full NHL season. So they were ready.

Craig, of course, would be the starting goalie. The defense was led by Bill Baker, Ken Morrow, Mike Ramsey, and Bob Suter. Joining Johnson and Eruzione at forward were the likes of Dave Christian, whose father and uncle had both been on the 1960 U.S. team; Steve Christoff, John Harrington, Rob McClanahan, Mark Pavelich, Buzz Schneider, Dave Silk, and Phil Verchota. Some of the names undoubtedly sound familiar even to new hockey fans, since a number of the players have gone on to fine careers in the NHL.

But that was the last thing on their minds at Lake Placid. The Americans had to open against a very tough team from Sweden, a game that might well serve as a barometer for the rest of the Olympics. Many predicted the Swedes for a medal, either a silver or bronze. And when Sweden scored first at the 11:04

18

Jim Craig, the star goaltender for the 1980 United States Winter Olympics ice hockey team, holds the American flag minutes after team USA clinched the gold medal. (AP/Wide World Photo)

mark of the opening period, some thought the U.S. team would crumble.

Thanks to the goaltending of Jim Craig, however, the Americans hung in there. Craig stopped 15 Swedish shots in the opening session, and continued his hot play in the second period. Finally, with 28 seconds left in the second stanza, Dave Silk scored the tying goal for the U.S. team. But early in the third, the Swedes scored again for a 2–1 lead. Now the Americans would have to scramble for the tie.

"We were so high-strung before the game that we were this far from snapping," said Mike Ramsey afterward. "It would have been a real emotional letdown if we didn't get a point tonight. And the way we started out, well, I wasn't sure."

But as time continued to run down, the U.S. team still couldn't get the tying score. Finally, with less than a minute remaining, Brooks pulled goalie Craig and put an extra skater on the ice. Then with just 27 seconds left, defenseman Bill Baker slammed a 25-footer past Sweden's goaltender for the score. The game ended in a 2–2 deadlock.

Though it was only a tie, it was a morale victory. The team knew it could compete with the Europeans. But Coach Brooks wanted them to work even harder.

"I told them tonight," the coach said, "that anyone who wants to come to work for me better bring a lunch pail and a hard hat."

"The coach uses every tool he can to keep us psyched," said goalie Craig. "But I tell you, our performance tonight was not unexpected. We believed in us, and now maybe others will."

They had to be up, for their next game was against powerful Czechoslovakia. What happened that night really made believers of everyone. The Americans came out following their coach's advice to use their youth and enthusiasm, and they were all over the Czechs from the opening face-off. They hit the older, more experienced Europeans with bruising body checks, and their quick poke checks often stopped the Czechs from starting their fast rushes up ice.

The Americans also worked in close for good shots instead of firing long 60-footers. And when the game ended the U.S. team had a stunning, 7–3 upset victory. It was hard to believe. Now everyone, including the Russians, had to take notice of the team of young Americans who seemed to be peaking at just the right time.

"We wanted to win so bad," said Mike Ramsey. "The feeling in the locker room was unbelievable. It was an emotional high, and the thought that we could stay that high for 60 minutes was great. After it ended, everyone was going around saying, 'Hey, we just upset the Czechs.'"

The way Olympic hockey is set up, the 12 competing teams were split into two divisions of 6 teams each. Then they play five games, with the top two teams in each division advancing to the medal round. The others are finished. With Sweden and Czechoslovakia in the same division, the Americans knew they couldn't afford to lose a game.

Following the two games came three easier ones. The Americans beat Norway 5–1, then topped Romania 7–2, and followed that with a 4–2 win over West Germany. After five games they were tied with the Swedes with identical 4–0–1 records. But the Swedes were awarded first place on the basis of goals scored. Both teams made it to the medal round, where the Russians and the team from Finland were waiting.

Had they finished first, the Americans would have met the Finns, then hopefully the Russians for the gold medal. But now they would be meeting the powerful Soviets in the first game of the medal round. It was to be an epic confrontation.

"We knew we'd have to play them sooner or later," Jim Craig said. "So now it looks like sooner. I think what they'll do is take a lot of shots early and try to break us quick. We can't let that happen. And if it does, I have to try to stop them."

The Americans remembered how their lack of checking in the 10–3 Garden defeat hurt them. They knew they'd have to hit harder and more often. Before the Olympics began, Herb Brooks had said he would be very surprised if the Russians didn't win the gold medal. He told reporters he was hoping for a bronze for his team. But anyone who knew Brooks knew what he really wanted. Anything less than a gold would be a disappointment. That's just the way he was made.

With the tension building as game time approached, perhaps it was goalie Craig who reduced everything to its simplest terms.

"If they beat us, it means they're better. If we beat

them, it means we're better. That's really all there is to it."

The intensity was everywhere as the two teams prepared to square off. In their bright red uniforms, the Russians looked like a formidable lot. They came out flying, and as Craig had predicted, taking shots at him whenever they had the chance. But the goaltender showed that he wasn't about to wilt under the pressure and neither did his teammates.

Still, it was the Russians who got the first score, slamming one home at the 9:12 mark of the first period. Now came a crucial time for the Americans. Were the Russians to score quickly again, it could signal the end. But the U.S. players dug in, skated and checked even harder, and at the 14:03 mark Buzz Schneider got the Americans even, scoring on an assist from Mark Pavelich.

That was the big one. Even when the Russians again took the lead with a score at the 17:34 mark, the Americans now felt they could come back, that they could skate with their Soviet counterparts. And they didn't stop skating, the proof being that Mark Johnson tied the game again just one second before the buzzer sounded ending the period. Dave Christian and Dave Silk had the assists, and the Americans left the ice knowing the match was tied. The Russians left knowing they were in for a tough game.

"I was just trying to keep us in the game," goalie Craig said of his performance in the first period. "The Russians hadn't been beaten and we knew they would play with a lot of class. I was ready for anything, because every shot in a game like this is a very big shot."

The Russians controlled play for much of the second period. In fact, they got the go-ahead goal early, at the 2:18 mark, but with a 3–2 lead they pressed for the advantage, and didn't really get it. The Americans tightened up defensively, checking well and keeping the Russians from getting any breakaways. And when they did get a shot, Jim Craig was there to turn it away.

At the outset of the third and final period the Russians still held that slim, 3–2 lead. But the fact that they couldn't extend it was significant. It was as if there was a feeling in the air. The tension was building. The next goal, if there was one, could be the biggest of the games.

It was Mark Johnson who finally got it. It came at the 8:39 mark as Johnson beat the Russian goaltender with a quick shot to tie the score at 3–3. Now, with some 11 minutes of hockey left, the game was again up for grabs. The fans who had jammed the field house at Lake Placid were in an uproar, and the millions of fans glued to their television sets at home were also on the edges of their seats.

And they didn't have long to wait. Just over a minute after Johnson's goal the Americans struck again. This time it was captain Mike Eruzione. He swiped the puck as the Russians were trying to clear it and fired a beautiful wrist shot past the startled Soviet netminder. Eruzione was mobbed by his teammates and the fans screamed even louder. The go-ahead score had come at exactly the halfway mark in the session. There were

24

still 10 minutes of hockey left. And if the Americans had scored a pair of goals in 81 seconds, the Russians could do it as well. With just a 4–3 lead, the Americans knew the game wasn't over as yet.

With everyone holding their collective breaths the two teams continued to battle. Every time the Russians managed to get the puck into the United States end, someone was there to kick it out. And if they did get a shot, Craig was there to make the stop. And the seconds continued to tick away. Could the impossible be happening?

The Russians tried and tried again. But they couldn't score. With less than a minute left the roar was deafening. Now there were seconds remaining. Five . . . four . . . three . . . two . . .

And as the clock went to one TV announcer Al Michaels beat the buzzer by saying his now famous line:

"Do you believe in miracles?"

The United States had won it. Their 4–3 win had pinned the first Olympic loss on a Russian hockey team in 12 years. At the buzzer, the entire American team mobbed goalie Craig, who had turned away 36 Russian shots.

"Jimmy Craig told me yesterday, 'You wait, coach; just wait and see what we do to these guys,' " Brooks said. "I told him he was crazy. But to play the way we did we had to have a strong goalie back there. Jimmy showed what he was made of tonight."

Though the celebration was loud and long, it wasn't over yet. The Americans still had one more game, against Finland, and they had to win that one to get the gold medal. That gave Coach Brooks one more psych job. He didn't want his team to suffer a big letdown after beating the Russians. The Finns could be very tough.

It looked that way in the opening period. Finland got the only score at the 9:20 mark when Jukka Porvari slapped a 35-footer past Craig. The 1–0 lead stood up until 4:39 of the second period when Steve Christoff beat the Finnish goaltender for a goal. But some two minutes later Mikko Leinonen beat Craig to give the Finns the lead once more. And they still had that 2–1 lead when the second period ended. But the Americans were still confident. They had been coming back during the entire Olympics.

"The third period has been our best throughout the tournament," Rob McClanahan said. "We knew coming out for the third we were smoking. No way they were gonna stop us."

Mike Ramsey echoed those sentiments. "Coming this far," the defenseman said, "there was no way we weren't gonna wrap up the gold."

And they started making good on their promise. A little over two minutes into the final session Phil Verchota tied the game after taking a pass from Dave Christian. Three minutes and 40 seconds later, Rob McClanahan got the go-ahead score on passes from Christian and Mark Johnson. And with just 3:35 left in the game and the United States team a man short, Johnson sewed it up with a nifty goal that put the icing on the cake.

26

Forward Mark Johnson raises his hands over the fallen Finnish goaltender as he scores the fourth and final goal in the USA's 4–2 gold medal–clinching win over Finland. (AP/Wide World Photo)

During the final 13 minutes of the game the U.S. team played shorthanded nearly half the time because of penalties. Yet the Finns could manage just a single shot on goal. The others were all blocked or smothered by the Americans, who seemed to be all over the ice.

"My men were diving, blocking them with their bodies, blocking them with their head, with anything," goalie Craig said.

And then it was over. They had done it. The Americans had won the gold medal, had performed a miracle on ice. They mobbed each other, thrusting their index fingers in the air to show they were number one. And goalie Craig, an American flag draped around him, searched the stands for his father so he could share his greatest moment.

There would be more celebrating, a visit to the White House, and the adulation of the entire nation. Then the players would go their separate ways. Some would become pros immediately, to varying degrees of success. Others would return to school. Still others would enter the real world, and decide what they wanted to do with the rest of their lives.

"I think we'd still like to play together," said Captain Eruzione, who would forever be remembered for his winning goal against the Russians. Eruzione had already announced he would not try to play professional hockey.

"We all came together six months ago," he continued, "from different backgrounds and different ethnic beliefs. And we made ourselves a team. There's nobody on this team from Boston; there's nobody on this team from Minnesota. Everyone here is from the Olympic Village."

It was truly a team effort, one that will never be forgotten. The 1980 United States ice hockey team wasn't supposed to win. They weren't supposed to beat the Russians. They just weren't good enough.

The problem was that someone forgot to tell them that.

Two Series, Two Upsets

Upsets happen. If they didn't, sports wouldn't be quite the same. But the thing that makes upsets so special is that they're never really expected and no one knows when they are going to occur. Sometimes years can pass in a certain sport or a particular event with no great upsets in the offing.

But then again, there are times when upsets occur with surprisingly frequency. The old adage "May the best team win," certainly doesn't always apply to sports. Although there is sometimes a great deal of room for argument about which is the best team under a particular set of circumstances.

On two occasions in recent years there have been very unusual kinds of upsets in one of the country's most watched and talked about sporting events—the World Series. It happened in 1985 and again in 1987.

The first unusual circumstance is that the same National League team, the St. Louis Cardinals, was the victim of the upset in both cases. Both times the Cards were preseries favorites, and on each occasion it looked at one point as if they were destined to win. But they didn't.

In 1985, the St. Louis Cardinals seemed to be the best team in baseball. They won over 100 games during the regular season and were a team with a balance of pitching, speed, and power. They had a lineup of all-stars, players like first baseman Jack Clark, second basemen Tommy Herr, shortstop Ozzie Smith, center-fielder Willie McGee, and rookie leftfielder Vince Coleman.

On the mound they had a pair of 20-game winners in lefty John Tudor and righty Joaquin Andujar, some solid secondary starters, and a strong bullpen. They also had a manager in Whitey Herzog who was considered by many the shrewdest in the game. It surprised no one when the Cards made it into the World Series, and were installed as immediate favorites to win.

Their opponents would be the surprising Kansas City Royals. The Royals, under manager Dick Howser, had won the American League West with a 91–71 record, not the kind of mark that champions are always made of. And in the American League playoffs the Royals went up against the Toronto Blue Jays, who were favored to win.

It was the first year that the playoffs had been moved from a best of five series to a best of seven. Had it still been a best of five, the Jays would have won. They took three of the first four games and seemed a shoe-in. But, miraculously, the Royals came back, and to the surprise of nearly everyone they swept three straight games to win 4–3, and earn themselves a trip to the fall classic, where the Cards would be waiting.

Kansas City did not have a bad team. They were led by one of the game's best hitters in George Brett, and had other fine players, such as Willie Wilson, Frank White, and Hal McRae. In addition, they had some fine pitchers, beginning with 21-year-old Bret Saberhagen, who won 20 games, Charlie Leibrandt, and Bud Black, as well as one of the best relief pitchers in the game, Dan Quisenberry. But somehow, they did not seem in the same class with the Cards.

Before the series started the Cardinals suffered a loss when their rookie leftfielder, Vince Coleman, who had stolen more than 100 bases, injured a leg in a freak accident during practice when one of the tarps that cover the field was rolled out onto his leg. He would miss the entire series.

But the Cards were National League batting and scoring champions, a fact that could not be overlooked, Coleman or no Coleman. And when they won the first two games at Kansas City, the odds, already in their favor, skyrocketed. There were certainly a couple of good reasons for this.

For one thing, going into the ninth inning of game two, the Royals held a 2–0 lead with Charlie Leibrandt on the mound. To that point, Leibrandt was pitching a two-hit shutout. But by the time the Royals got the

Cards out, they had pushed across four runs, several coming in on bloop hits, to pull the game out, 4–2. It was a heartbreaking defeat that could have easily demoralized the K.C. team.

In addition, a look at the history books showed that no team had ever come back to win a World Series after dropping the first two games at home. So to win, the Royals would have to make baseball history. And that doesn't happen every day.

Then in game three, Kansas City started young Bret Saberhagen, and even though he won 20 games in the regular season, he had to be something of a question mark. Oakland had knocked him out of the box in the next-to-last game of the season, and in the third game of the playoffs against Toronto, he had been hit on the foot by a line drive and then got creamed after that.

So as Saberhagen took the mound to face the Cards on their home turf at St. Louis, he knew he had to win. For another statistic showed that no team had ever come back from a 3–0 deficit to win the series. The odds against the Royals were high enough. They didn't need still another mountain to climb.

But could Saberhagen concentrate on the game? He was just 21 years old and his wife was back in Kansas City expecting their first child at any time. Yet he seemed anything but nervous when he told the press, "What we [the Royals] are is relaxed and confident."

Strong words with his team trailing by two games, but Saberhagen was ready to back up his words with deeds. He went out and pitched a brilliant game, holding the Cards to just six hits as he went all the way in a

6–1 K.C. victory. The youngster was poised and polished as he struck out eight Cardinals and walked only one. He had gotten his club back in it—but for how long?

Not too long, perhaps. For the next night Redbird ace John Tudor took the mound and hurled a five-hit shutout, supported by home runs off the bats of Tito Landrum and Willie McGee. Tudor's win gave the Cardinals a 3–1 bulge in the series. So the odds were still against the Royals. Only five teams in the long history of the World Series had come back to win after being down 3–1, the last being the 1979 Pittsburgh Pirates. With one game left in St. Louis, the Cards were hoping to clinch at home.

A Cardinal victory seemed such a sure bet that the television people were already constructing a platform in the Royals' clubhouse so the losers could be interviewed.

"They're getting ready for all the long faces," quipped Frank White. And young Saberhagen, still loose, only laughed and said, "They've fallen right into our trap. We've got them where we want them."

If anything was in the Royals' favor, it was the specter of history repeating. They had been down 3–1 to the Blue Jays in the playoffs and had come back to win. So they knew it was possible. And if they had done it before, why not do it again?

There was very little suspense in game five. Willie Wilson slammed a two-run triple in the second inning, giving the Royals a lead they never relinquished. Operating behind the five-hit pitching of Danny Jackson,

Kansas City won easily, 6–1, extending the series at least one more day. But some people were already asking the question could they do it again, could they pull off another major upset?

The sixth game had all the high drama of a Shakespearean play. It was scoreless for seven innings, and as each inning passed without a run, the Royals knew that a sudden turn of events could end their dream within a matter of minutes. And that's what it looked like would happen in the top of the eighth when the Cards pushed across a run off Charlie Leibrandt on a bloop single by pinch hitter Brian Harper. Now the Royals had just six outs left. And after they went down harmlessly in the eighth, they had only three remaining.

More stats. The Cardinals had not blown a ninth-inning lead all season long and no team had ever rallied in the ninth from the brink of elimination to win the series. Plus the Cards now had ace reliever Todd Worrell on the mound. It looked bleak.

Jorge Orta led off as a pinch hitter and with a two-strike count hit a squibbler off the end of his bat. First baseman Jack Clark fielded the ball and flipped to the covering Worrell. The first-base umpire called Orta safe and the Cards argued vehemently. They felt Worrell had beaten him to the bag.

But the call stood. Big Steve Balboni was up next and, after Clark failed to catch his foul pop, singled to left. Jim Sundberg tried to bunt the runners over, but Orta was forced at third. Hal McRae was now at bat. But a passed ball allowed the runners to move up and

McRae was intentionally walked to load the bases. Now up came another pinch hitter, lefty Dane Iorg.

"It's a situation you dream about as a child," said Iorg, "coming to the plate in the bottom of the ninth inning with the bases loaded and a World Series game on the line."

Coming up is one thing, producing is another. But Iorg produced, blooping a base hit to right field, and as the tying and winning runs crossed the plate the fans in Kansas City went wild. Their team had won it, and now there would be a seventh game for all the marbles.

It would be a battle of aces, Bret Saberhagen against John Tudor. And before the game, Tudor, who had gone 20–2 after a 1–6 start, said a strange thing.

"There's something in me that would love to pitch this game," he said. "But as I sit here, I'd rather not pitch it . . . there's always that feeling deep down inside that if I should lose it would ruin the whole season."

As for Saberhagen, he was on cloud nine. His wife had just given birth to a son and he couldn't have been happier. Asked about the possibility of his losing, he said, "How could I be disappointed about anything? We've had a great season and I've had a great season and I'm a father."

Like so many final games, this one was anticlimactic. Saberhagen had his good stuff and Tudor didn't. Rightfielder Darryl Motley started things off for K.C. with a two-run homer in the second inning and the rout was on. By the time Tudor left after just two and one-third innings, the Royals had a 5–0 lead and they kept

36

Young Bret Saberhagen of the Royals was the pitching star of the series, winning two games, including the seventh and deciding one. (Courtesy Kansas City Royals)

pouring it on from there to the delight of their screaming fans.

When it ended, K.C. had an 11–0 victory, as
Saberhagen had pitched a brilliant, five-hit shutout to
earn the Most Valuable Player prize. What's more, the
Royals had made history by becoming the first team to
win a world series after losing the first two games at
home. Their pitchers had held the Cards to just 13 runs
in seven games, and the St. Louis players had swiped
just two bases after pilfering 310 during the regular
season.

Happy days were here again in Kansas City, and all
because of one of the big upsets in World Series history.

Two years later the Cardinals were back and favored
to win the fall classic once more. But in some ways
history was repeating. For one thing, they would be
playing the Minnesota Twins, an American League
Western Division team that had the poorest record of
any of the four playoff clubs, and that was similar to
the Royals in '85.

In addition, they had once again lost a star player to
injury. This time it was Jack Clark, their power-hitting
first basemen. Clark had a severely injured ankle and
couldn't play. Still, the Cards were the favorites because they had played so well during the regular season
and had fought off a challenge by the defending champion New York Mets.

Though they weren't the same team they had been in
'85, St. Louis still had some fine pitching and a great

deal of team speed. With Clark out, they would be hurting for long-ball power, but they had been a better team than Minnesota all season long. And in the play-offs they had shown a great deal of character by coming back from a 3–2 deficit to defeat the San Francisco Giants in seven games.

Minnesota was the surprise team of 1987. They had taken the American League West title with fewer than 90 victories (85–77), an unusual occurrence, and while they were very tough in their home park, they had an extremely difficult time winning ballgames on the road.

But the Twins were a very dangerous offensive ball-team, with the likes of Kirby Puckett, Gary Gaetti, Kent Hrbek, and Tom Brunansky. They also had a pair of outstanding starting pitchers in Frank Viola and Bert Blyleven, as well as a bullpen stopper in Jeff Reardon. In addition, they were solid defensively and had what many people considered an extra player—the Metrodome itself.

The Hubert H. Humphrey Metrodome was one of the toughest parks in the majors for visiting teams. Some of the Twins' opponents complained about the playing surface, the lighting, and the noise. Most of all the noise. Filled with rabid Minnesota fans, the noise in the Metrodome could be deafening. And many felt it was the roar of the crowd that caused opposing teams to lose concentration and thus ballgames. In the play-offs, the Twins easily defeated the favored Detroit Tigers, four games to one, and advanced to the series, which was slated to open at the Dome.

Frank Viola was manager Tom Kelly's choice to

With two big victories over the Cards, lefthander
Frank Viola was named the Most Valuable Player in the
1987 World Series. (Courtesy Minnesota Twins)

open on the mound, while Herzog, still juggling his rotation after the long playoff series with the Giants, was forced to go with young lefthander Joe Magrane. Yet it was the Cardinals who drew first blood in the second inning when Jim Lindeman doubled, went to third on a fly out, and scored on a grounder to short.

The 1–0 lead held up into the Minnesota fourth, and that's when the pattern for the entire series unfolded with swift and thunderous suddenness. Gaetti opened the inning with an infield single. Designated hitter Don Baylor followed with a base hit and Brunansky singled to load the bases.

Kent Hrbek then followed with a fourth consecutive base hit to drive in two runs. A walk to Steve Lombardozzi loaded the bases again and Bob Forsch relieved Magrane. Forsch was greeted by a Tim Laudner single that drove home another run. That brought up left-fielder Dan Gladden.

Forsch pitched and Gladden drove the ball to deep centerfield. Willie McGee could only watch it sail into the seats for a grand slam home run as the crowd at the Metrodome went berserk. The Twins had erupted for seven runs and the game was all but over. The final score was 10–0 and the Twins were on their way.

The next night it was more of the same. St. Louis started Danny Cox against Bert Blyleven. This time the Twins got a run in the second, and once again in the bottom of the fourth they erupted. This time they tallied six times to take a 7–0 lead as Tim Laudner and Gary Gaetti blasted home runs. From there, the Twins coasted to an 8–4 win and a 2–0 lead in the series.

"We're on a mission," said Gaetti after the game. "At least in the Dome. This is what we've been doing all year here. I would expect they'll have the advantage in their place like we do in ours."

Gaetti might not have realized at the time, but he was actually being a prophet. The Twins now had to travel to Busch Stadium in St. Louis. And if the past was any indication, they would now be in trouble. For in 1987, including the playoffs and first two games of the World Series, Minnesota had a 60–25 record at the Metrodome, but only a 31–53 log on the road. They were really like two different teams.

"We were underdogs against the Tigers and we're underdogs now," said Manager Tom Kelly. "But some people are really just seeing us for the first time. If you pitch good and catch the ball, you've got a chance to win."

But in St. Louis, the Twins looked like a different team, an inept one, especially at the plate. Game three was scoreless for five innings, Cardinal ace John Tudor matching serves with rookie Les Straker of the Twins. Minnesota got a run in the sixth on a Brunanski single, but St. Louis came back in the seventh to score three times off reliever Juan Berenguer. Vince Coleman's double brought home a pair, and a single by Ozzie Smith got the third run home. Reliever Todd Worrell shut the Twins down in the final two frames to preserve the victory. The Cards were back in it.

Minnesota went back to Frank Viola in game four, while the Cards started Greg Mathews. Minnesota scored first on a solo homer by shortstop Greg Gagne, but in the fourth inning the Cards knocked out Viola, who was bothered by the cold, 42-degree temperature. The big hit was a three-run homer by little-used Tom Lawless, who was filling in for injured third sacker Terry Pendleton. The homer keyed a 6–2 Cardinal victory that tied the series at two games each.

"We were long overdue for a big inning," said centerfielder Willie McGee.

Then in the pivotal fifth game, the Cards did it again. This time they won by a 4–2 score to take a 3–2 lead in the series. Once again they assumed the favorite role. But there was still one thing they hadn't done, and unless they did it, they wouldn't win the World Series. The Cards still had to win a game in the Metrodome.

They tried again in game six, manager Herzog gambling by starting John Tudor with just three days rest. Tudor didn't have it, and the Twins once again stormed from behind, the big blow being a dramatic, grand slam home run by Kent Hrbek off reliever Ken Daley. With more than 55,000 fans screaming on every pitch, the Twins won it, 11–5, sending the series to a seventh and deciding game.

Now the Twins had their ace, Frank Viola, ready once more, while the Cards were forced to go with young Joe Magrane. Herzog's gamble in using Tudor in game six may have backfired. But to the surprise of everyone, it was the Cards who scored first, getting a pair of runs in the second with the RBIs coming off the bats of Tony Peña and Steve Lake.

But the Twins got one back in the second as Steve Lombardozzi singled home Tom Brunansky. Viola had apparently settled down, and in the fifth Minnesota tied it on a Greg Gagne single and double by Kirby Puckett off reliever Danny Cox, who had come into the game with only two days' rest. Now the fans were roaring with anticipation on every pitch.

The go-ahead run came home in the sixth when Brunansky walked, Hrbek walked, and with one out Roy Smalley walked, loading the bases. After Gladden struck out against reliever Todd Worrell, Gagne got an infield single, scoring Brunansky before Worrell pitched out of the inning.

With Viola still coasting along, the Twins got an insurance tally in the eighth. It came home on a Laudner single and double by Gladden. The Twins were now three outs away, and closer Jeff Reardon came on and calmly retired the Cardinals in the ninth. The Twins had done it. They had upset the Cards to become world champions!

What a strange series it had been. It was the first time in baseball history that the home team had won all seven games of a World Series. And what a difference. In the four games at the Metrodome the Twins hitters were 46 for 140, a .329 average. In the three games at Busch Stadium, those same hitters were just 18 for 98 and a .184 mark. By contrast, the Cardinals pitchers had a 1.67 earned run average at Busch, yet it ballooned to an inflated 9.00 at the Metrodome.

The celebration in Minnesota was a wild one. The club had pulled off a mighty upset, and considering that just five years earlier the Twins had lost 102 games, they had really achieved something.

Minnesota first baseman Kent Hrbek slams a bases-loaded home run to break up the sixth game of the 1987 World Series. The Twins went on to upset the Cardinals in seven games. (Courtesy Minnesota Twins)

"I can't even begin to describe how far this organization has come," said Tom Brunansky, who was there in tougher times. "We were bad. Worse than bad. And look what we are now. World champions."

But to those critics who said it was the screaming fans in the Metrodome that won the series for the Twins, Manager Kelly answered quickly.

"We appreciate the fans and their support," he said. "They've been great and we love them. But it's the boys on the field who get the job done, not the fans. The boys are the ones who have to perform, to pitch, to hit, to field."

And that is really how upsets are made.

A Blaze of an Upset

He was one of the most electrifying performers in the history of college basketball, and he played for a team that ruled the collegiate ranks for a dozen years. The player was Bill Walton, the 6'11" redhead who played center for the UCLA Bruins from 1972–74.

With Walton anchoring the middle and surrounded by a supporting cast of outstanding players, the Bruins won an incredible 88 straight games and a pair of NCAA championships. Playing for the great John Wooden, Walton became a three-time all-American and the most heralded collegiate center since his predecessor at UCLA, Lew Alcindor, later known as Kareem Abdul-Jabbar.

When Walton graduated after the 1974 season, great things were predicted for him in the National Basketball Association. He seemed to have all the skills. He was a good shooter, outstanding rebounder, and one of the best passing centers of all time. In addition, he was a team player first, and an individual second.

The team that drafted him prior to the 1974–75 season was the Portland Trailblazers, a club with one of the poorest records in the NBA. Walton went to Portland, but he wasn't overjoyed. He said he didn't like the climate, the dampness and the rain, and expressed openly the desire to play in his native southern California. But he was a ballplayer and a competitor, and once on the court he played as hard as he ever did. The Blazers figured they had a franchise player, a center they could build around for the next decade.

Portland already had one former UCLA star in 6'9" forward Sidney Wicks. He was an NBA all-star, as was guard Geoff Petrie. So with Walton joining those two, the Blazers figured they had the nucleus of a winner. But there was one thing they hadn't counted on. At UCLA Bill Walton had been a healthy, durable player. At Portland, he suddenly became brittle.

Though he showed flashes of his former self as a rookie, leg and foot injuries held him to just 35 games. He averaged 12.8 points a game and grabbed 441 rebounds as the Blazers improved to 38–44. A full season from the big guy and the team most certainly would have been over .500.

A year later it was a little better. This time he played in 51 games and averaged 16.1 a game. But he still missed some 31 games and the Blazers again finished last in their division with a 37–45 mark. Then came 1976–77, Walton's third year, and a year in which another drama was being played out in the National Basketball Association.

The NBA had just completed a merger agreement with the rival American Basketball Association, which was on the brink of folding. The NBA absorbed four of the ABA's strongest franchises, taking in the Denver Nuggets, New York Nets, Indiana Pacers, and San Antonio Spurs. There were some fine players on these teams and they would all be welcome additions to the older league.

But there was one guy, in particular, that NBA fans were anxious to see. He was New York Nets forward Julius Erving, the man known as Doctor J. Erving was perhaps the most exciting player in the game. In the freewheeling style of the Nets, he electrified crowds everywhere with his variety of moves to the hoop, his leaping ability, and his seemingly impossible slam dunks. They called him the best one-on-one player in the game.

Only there was a problem. Doctor J wanted the Nets to renegotiate his contract and the team refused. The impasse continued and finally Erving said he would not report to training camp. The Nets didn't want the problem, and just before the season started they shocked the basketball world by shipping Erving to the Philadelphia 76ers, a team hungry for a championship.

Just two years earlier, the 76ers were in the Eastern Division basement, but in 1975–76 they had gone out and signed another former ABA star, 6'8" forward George McGinnis, considered one of the best in the game. With McGinnis averaging 23 points and grabbing nearly 1,000 rebounds in his first NBA season, the Sixers improved to 46–36, but were eliminated in the first round of the playoffs.

Now, with Erving joining McGinnis, the team was talking title. They had some fine supporting players in centers Caldwell Jones and Darryl Dawkins, guards Doug Collins and Lloyd Free, and backup forward Steve Mix. The question was whether the two super-star forwards could share the same court.

They could, with part of the reason being Erving's unselfishness. He completely toned down the free-wheeling running style he had played with the Nets, and became part of a team concept, which more than justified the anticipation shown by Doug Collins when he heard the Doctor would arrive in Philly.

"I'm just so excited," Collins said. "I just can't imagine playing on the same team with George and Julius. The thought of the excitement we could create on the court is beyond my imagination right now."

With the two superstars both averaging over 21 points a game, the Sixers improved to a division leading 50–32 record. Only the Los Angeles Lakers had a better mark in the entire league, and it was thought that Philly had as good a chance as anyone to win the league title.

Meanwhile, things were also happening out at Portland, where Bill Walton missed some games early in the season, but then began playing as he had at UCLA. The team had added a young power forward, Maurice Lucas, from the ABA, and had developed a fine floor

This is how the great Bill Walton looked when he led the Portland Trailblazers to the NBA title in 1977. (Courtesy Portland Trailblazers)

leader in guard Lionel Hollins. Once Walton was healthy, the Blazers showed they could play with anyone.

They finished the regular season just four games behind the Lakers in the Pacific Division with a 49–33 record. And Walton had finally lived up to his advance notices. He was second behind Lucas in team scoring with an 18.6 average, and playing in 65 games, he led the NBA in rebounding with a 14.4 average, and in blocked shots with 3.25 a game.

Yet despite Portland's strong finish, the Lakers with Kareem Abdul-Jabbar, and the 76ers with Erving and McGinnis, were considered the most likely candidates to play for the championship.

In the first round of the playoffs, the Blazers had to go three games to eliminate the Chicago Bulls, 2–1. They then moved into the semifinals, where Walton and Lucas led them past the Denver Nuggets, four games to two. Now they would meet the Lakers for the Western Conference crown.

Philadelphia, in the meantime, had drawn a bye in the first round, then went up against their old rivals, the Boston Celtics, in the semifinals. The series went the full seven games, but the Sixers finally won it, taking the last game by an 83–77 score. They were now in the Eastern Conference finals against the Houston Rockets and on a possible collision course with Walton and the Blazers.

And that's just the way it happened. Philly bested Houston in six games, while the Blazers did even better. They completely dominated and stunned the proud Lakers, beating them in four straight as Bill Walton outplayed Kareem Abdul-Jabbar. But even with Walton at the top of his game, the 76ers were favorites to take the NBA crown.

The series opened in Philadelphia and it was the Doctor's show, with some strong support from Doug Collins. Erving had 33 points, Collins 30, as the Sixers took the opener, 107–101. Even though George McGinnis had an off-game, Philly played well and the young Blazers seemed to feel the pressure. Portland turned the ball over 34 times, leading to 26 Sixer points. And with Doug Collins scoring so well, Lionel Hollins seemed to lose his concentration. And after the game, Bill Walton refused to make excuses.

"It's no different than the regular season," he said. "It's just basketball. I'm not gonna make excuses. They played better and they won. That's what counts. That's what we came to do and didn't."

No one could fault Walton, however. The big guy had 28 points and 20 rebounds. That should have been a warning. He was looking awfully unstoppable. But it was up to all the Blazers to regroup for game two, and some 18,276 fans jammed into the Philadelphia Spectrum to hope that they wouldn't. They didn't leave disappointed. Game two gave them a little of everything they wanted.

For one thing, the 76ers played outstanding team basketball. They scored the final five points of the first quarter to break a 26–26 deadlock. And then in the second session they extended that five-point lead to 18. That, in effect, finished the disorganized Blazers right then and there. No matter how hard they tried they couldn't get back in the game again.

During the second session, Philly got eight of its hoops on easy lay-ups, while the Blazers shot just 22 percent and turned the ball over seven times. They were looking more and more like a young and inexperienced team that just couldn't cope with the playoff pressure.

With that big halftime cushion, the Sixers coasted to a 107–89 victory, a game marked by a near fight between Philly's Darryl Dawkins and Portland's Maurice Lucas. But the big news was the ease with which the Sixers had won the game.

"People think we're a bunch of renegades," said Julius Erving, who scored 20 points. "They think a well-drilled team can come in here and pick us apart. Well, we're proving them wrong."

"That second period was a classic example of how to run the fast break," crowed George McGinnis. "The big guys got it off the boards, gave it to the little people, and then the big guys filled the lanes."

All Portland coach Jack Ramsay could say was that his team had "not played poised basketball. They're beating us because of our ineffective offense."

So the 76ers had a commanding, 2–0 lead in games as the teams traveled back to Portland for the third contest. It would be difficult for any team to come back from a two-game deficit. And since the Blazers were a young team that hadn't really played together for more than a season, it seemed the task would be doubly difficult. Portland now had to be considered big under-

Maurice Lucas was perhaps the toughest power forward in the league when the Blazers won the NBA title
over Philadelphia in a surprising upset. (Courtesy Portland Trailblazers)

dogs, and if they lost the pivotal third game, they would be all but out of it.

Perhaps the first ten minutes of the ballgame were the most important of the entire championship series. For in that brief span the young Blazers proved to themselves that they could play with the Sixers—in fact, could outplay them.

Roaring out of the gate at top speed, Portland raced to an incredible 32–12 lead in those first minutes. Philly bounced back to close the gap to 34–21 at the quarter, then to 60–53 at the half. If they could come back after intermission and win the game, that would just about finish the Blazers.

But this time Portland wasn't about to let that happen. Though the Sixers had the lead down to a scant two points during the third period, Portland had a five-point advantage going into the final 12 minutes of the game. Early in the period Philly had cut the lead to four, but then Walton hit on two straight difficult shots to bring it up to eight.

With Walton's baskets serving as a catalyst, the Blazers went on another run, similar to the opening of the game. They ended up with a 26–10 spurt that brought the lead right back up to 20 points, and then they coasted in from there, winning the game by a 129–107 margin. The 12,923 screaming Blazer fans were delighted. Their team had played itself right back into the series.

"That's our game," Jack Ramsay said. "Aggressive defense that triggers our offense. We didn't do it well in the first two games, but we did here, and we'll strive to do it again in game four."

Philadelphia Coach Gene Shue might have sounded a warning to his team when he said, "I don't think our team was flat. They're just very tough to beat on their court, and they got off to a good lead, which is something I didn't want to happen."

Lucas with 27 points and 12 rebounds, and Walton with 20 points, 18 rebounds, and nine assists led the Blazers. But they had great balance as well. Forward Bobby Gross had 19, while guards Johnny Davis and Lionel Hollins had 18 and 15 points respectively. The question was which Blazer team would come out for game four?

The answer came early. Once again, the Blazers blew the Sixers off the floor in the opening minutes. The teams traded baskets in the early going. But that 2–2 tie would be the only close score of the night. Just five minutes later it was a 21–6 game, and the Blazers were never threatened after that. At one point the lead was as high as 40 points, and when it ended, Portland had tied the series with a 130–98 victory.

"They truly embarrassed us," said Sixer guard Doug Collins. "They ran all over us in front of millions of people."

Suddenly it was a series, a real dogfight, and Philly knew it was in trouble. But they had one consolation. The key fifth game would be played at the Spectrum, as the two teams flew east once again. And as one Philadelphia writer pointed out, the Sixers had won all their "must" games during the season, and they had not lost three straight times all year long.

Game five followed a familiar pattern. Though neither team was shooting exceptionally well, the Blazers took an early lead, which reached seven points at the quarter. Philly came back in the second period to slice it to four at the half, 45–41. The difference, however, was that Portland continued to play a balanced game on both offense and defense, while Philly relied on Erving and Collins for the brunt of their scoring. Both George McGinnis and Lloyd Free continued to be mired in inexplicable shooting slumps.

Early in the third quarter the Sixers closed to 53–52, with McGinnis on the foul line shooting for the tie. But he missed the free throw, Walton got the rebound, and in less than four minutes the Blazers had made still another run that boosted the lead back to double figures.

The lead was up to 19 at the end of the third quarter. Philly gave its fans a little to cheer about in the final session when they made something of a run, but they fell six points short and lost, 110–104. Erving led all scorers with 37 points, while Collins had 23. But they were done in by the Portland balance.

Gross led the Blazers with 25 points, while Lucas had 20, Dave Twardzik 16, Walton and Hollins 14 each, and Davis 11. In addition Walton had 24 big rebounds. His presence underneath was as intimidating as any center's in the league, and reminiscent of the Bill Russell–Wilt Chamberlain days. Now the teams were re-

It was guard Lionel Hollins who often teamed with Walton and Lucas to trigger the fast-breaking offense that helped defeat the 76ers. (Courtesy Portland Trailblazers)

turning to Portland once again with the Blazers having a chance to clinch the title.

Only one other team (the 1969 Boston Celtics) had ever come from a 2–0 deficit in a final series to win. Thirteen others had tried and failed. In addition, the Blazers were seeking to become the first and only team since the 1949 Minneapolis Lakers to win an NBA crown in their first ever trip to the playoffs. Suddenly the underdogs were about to make history.

Blazermania had taken over the city of Portland, as more than 5,000 fans greeted their team's return in the middle of the night. Now some 12,000 fans would once again be squeezed into Memorial Coliseum as the Blazers tried to wrap up their first NBA crown in only their seventh season of existence.

The game turned out to be a real battle. In the first quarter, both teams played evenly. Portland was again playing with great balance, while Philly was depending mainly on Erving and George McGinnis, who had finally broken out of his playoff slump. When the buzzer sounded, the game was deadlocked at 27. But Blazer fans waited patiently for their team to make one of the runs that had characterized their three previous winning efforts.

It came in the second quarter this time. Combining Walton's defense and rebounding with a controlled fastbreak, the Blazers outscored Philly, 40–28, to take a solid, 67–55 lead at the half. And with the way the series had gone, many of their fans thought their heroes would coast all the way home. But in the third quarter the Sixers began clawing back, coming within nine. And in the final session, with the championship possibly on the line, they continued to come at the Blazers.

With six minutes left, the Blazers still had a solid, 12-point lead. Yet, led by Erving and McGinnis, the Sixers continued to cut the lead. With 2:20 remaining, the lead was at eight, 108–100. But a pair of baskets by the Doctor and a foul shot by Free cut the margin to just three points, 108–105. And suddenly Portland couldn't score. There was an offensive foul against Walton and then a couple of turnovers. Were the Blazers about to blow it?

At the 1:09 mark, Lucas hit a free throw to make it 109–105. With the tension mounting, both teams continued to battle. McGinnis hit a basket with just 18 seconds left, reducing the margin to 109–107. Then after Portland inbounded, McGinnis tied up Bob Gross and won the ensuing jump ball.

With seconds left, Erving missed a 20-foot jumper from out front that would have tied it. But Free grabbed the offensive rebound and took a shot from the baseline that also could have tied it. But he, too, missed. Still, Philadelphia retained possession, and with time running out, McGinnis had one last shot to knot it up. But he, too, missed, and the buzzer sounded, giving the Portland Trailblazers the NBA title.

It had been a great series, but in the end it was Portland's balance that won for them. Julius Erving had been brilliant in the final game with 40 points, while McGinnis chipped in with 28. But on the Portland side, Gross had 24, Hollins and Walton 20 each, Lucas 15, and Davis 13. In addition, Walton had 23 rebounds, seven assists, and eight big blocks. He was named the series' Most Valuable Player.

"I feel good all over," Walton said when it was over. And when someone asked if the NBA title was better than his NCAA titles at UCLA, Walton answered yes very quickly.

"This championship involves all the best players in this country, playing in one league. And with the merger it's truly the first championship of all the United States. And we won the first one like it."

Blazer coach Jack Ramsay was quick to laud his entire team. "This is the finest team and the finest people I've ever coached," he said. "This is what I've aimed for ever since becoming a professional coach. But I would feel the same way and say the same thing about these players even if we hadn't won."

It was a great victory, all right. And because of the fragile health of Bill Walton, it would not be repeated. The next year Walton was in the process of leading the Blazers to the best record in the NBA when he was injured in the 60th game. The team was 50–10 at the time, but without Walton finished at 58–24 and lost in the semifinals to Seattle.

But when healthy, Walton had proved he was one of the best. And he led his young team back from a 2–0 deficit against a veteran Philadelphia team that had been a heavy favorite. However, as in all sports, the underdog can never be fully counted out. The 1977 Portland Trailblazers proved that all over again.

Guaranteed Upset

It seems so long ago now that it's almost as if it never happened. In some ways you'd even expect the story to begin with "Once upon a time." But it did happen. Oh, did it ever. And when football fans talk about it today, they still call it the greatest upset in the history of the National Football League.

That's because it happened in the Super Bowl, Super Bowl III to be exact. It was the year the upstart New York Jets of the American Football League, led by a brash young quarterback named Joe Namath, toppled the powerful Baltimore Colts, the NFL team considered the best in football during the 1968 season.

Actually, it never would have happened had it not been for the creation of the American Football League, which began play in 1960 amid laughter and ridicule from the older league.

But by the mid-1960s the AFL had captured enough first-line talent to field some fine football teams, and the price war that resulted from the quest for talent was hurting both leagues. More and more it seemed as if the only solution was a merger, a joining of the two leagues into a bigger and better National Football League.

The merger was officially announced in June of 1966, a step-by-step process that began with a common draft of collegians in 1967, interleague preseason games that same year, and a full merger into one league in 1970.

But there was something else. The two leagues also decided to institute a new, AFL-NFL world championship game immediately, beginning after the 1966 season. It was a game that would become known as the Super Bowl, and before long it would be perhaps the single most glamorous event in the world of sports.

That's not what it was in those early days, however. Back then, it was the vehicle National Football League diehards had been waiting for. Now they could prove once and for all that their league was the stronger of the two, that the AFL was still composed of pretenders, upstarts who needed the older NFL to survive. And, indeed, when the legendary Vince Lombardi and his Green Bay Packers won the first two Super Bowls by the convincing scores of 35–10 over the Kansas City Chiefs, and 33–14 over the Oakland Raiders, it did appear that the NFL still had the stronger teams.

Then came the 1968 season. That year the Colts took over for the Packers as the National Football League powerhouse. Winning 13 of 14 games, Baltimore swept the NFL title, whipping the Cleveland Browns in the championship game by the decisive score of 34–0. No matter which team the AFL sent against them in the Super Bowl, the Colts would be heavy favorites. To many, they were unbeatable.

But in the American League another story was beginning to unfold. The New York Jets were emerging as one of the best teams in the league. That in itself attracted attention, because the Jets' quarterback attracted attention. He was Joe Namath, a strong-armed passer out of the University of Alabama, who signed with the Jets in 1965 for the then unheard-of sum of $400,000, the figure being the result of the price war between the two leagues.

But Namath turned out to be as flamboyant as he was talented. Despite playing on fragile knees, Joe Willie had become one of the best quarterbacks in the AFL. In 1967 he had thrown for 4,007 yards and the following year led the Jets to an 11–3 record and first-place finish in the AFL East. A thrilling, 27–23 victory over the defending champ Raiders gave the Jets the league title and put them into the Super Bowl.

Though the Colts were made overwhelming favorites, with the point spread fluctuating between 18 and 23, it was Joe Namath who began to garner most of the publicity. Namath was a love-him or hate-him kind of guy. He had become known as "Broadway Joe" for his high-profile life-style in New York.

Often seen in public with a variety of beautiful women, Namath seemed to enjoy the life of a super-star. He wore fur coats in the winter, grew a "Fu

Manchu" mustache when facial hair still wasn't popular among athletes, and was often as quick with his mouth as he was with the forward pass.

But despite his off-field reputation, Joe Willie was all business on the gridiron. He was a courageous leader who often played in pain, and a smart quarterback who could spot a defensive weakness in a flash and pick it apart with his quick release of the football. Yet there were very few football fans anywhere who felt that Namath, or for that matter, any other quarterback, could possibly lead the Jets over the mighty Colts.

Baltimore had a legendary quarterback of its own in John Unitas. But he had been out of action with a sore arm, leaving the signal calling to the more-than-adequate Earl Morrall. Looking past the quarterback position, however, the team was stocked with good, tough football players.

The Colts had a solid offensive line and outstanding pass receivers in Jimmy Orr, Willie Richardson, and all-league tight end John Mackey. Tom Matte was a versatile halfback and Jerry Hill a dependable fullback. The defense was the heart of the team, led by linemen Bubba Smith and Billy Ray Smith, linebackers Mike Curtis and Dennis Gaubatz, and defensive backs Bobby Boyd and Rick Volk. In addition, the Baltimore bench was very strong.

To most NFL fans, the Jets were of unknown quantity. Namath, of course, was highly visible, but most of the others were not, and even if they had the stats, diehard NFL fans tended to ignore them because, they reasoned, the numbers were rung up against inferior

AFL opposition. Yet in looking back, it's now obvious that the 1968 New York Jets football team contained some very fine individual players.

Besides Namath, the offense featured a hard-running fullback in Matt Snell and a slippery halfback in Emerson Boozer. Speedy Don Maynard, tricky George Sauer, and tough Pete Lammons were a fine trio of receivers. And the offensive line with Winston Hill, Bob Talamini, John Schmitt, Randy Rasmussen, and Dave Herman, was outstanding.

Defensively, the Jets had a pair of fine defensive ends in Gerry Philbin and Verlon Biggs, an all-league tackle in John Elliott, quick linebackers in Ralph Baker, Al Atkinson, and Larry Grantham, and some solid defensive backs, led by safety Jim Hudson and ex Colt Johnny Sample. This club would not be intimidated by the Colts and their 18-point-favorites role.

Then as the game drew closer, Joe Namath began to run his mouth, and the Colts players started seething. Who did this 25-year-old kid think he was? And where did he get the nerve to say the things he was saying?

"I study quarterbacks," Namath said at one point. "And I can tell you that the Colts have never had to play against the kind of quarterbacks we have in the AFL. There are at least five AFL quarterbacks that I would rate over Earl Morrall."

Baltimore's huge defensive end, Bubba Smith, answered by saying that real good football players "don't have to talk. The Green Bay Packers were real champions and they never talked."

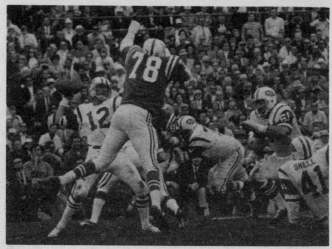

Broadway Joe shows his great passing form as the Colts' Bubba Smith (78) tries in vain to block Namath's toss. (AP/Wide World Photo)

But that didn't stop Namath. A week before the game he had a confrontation with several Baltimore players at a Miami restaurant when he told them flat out that the Jets would win the ballgame. For a few tense moments it looked as if a fight would break out. But then Namath paid everyone's tab by plunking a $100 bill on the bar.

As game time approached, the odds on the Colts continued to rise. Perhaps that's what prompted Namath to make the brashest statement yet. Asked once again if he really thought the Jets had a chance he turned and said, "We're going to win the game. I guarantee it!"

That was the last straw. Here was this kid in his fourth professional season and playing in the Super

Bowl on a team that was an 18-point underdog, and he was guaranteeing a victory. The Colts couldn't believe it. They vowed not only to win the game, but to give Joe Willie Namath a lesson he wouldn't forget.

There were more than 75,000 fans packed into the Orange Bowl in Miami on January 12, 1969, and millions more watching on television as the Jets took the field against the Colts. Memories of the two Green Bay victories still lingered, and some thought the Colts would win by an even greater margin than had the Packers.

Oh, yes. There was one more irony. The coach of the Jets was Weeb Ewbank, the same man who had once led the Colts to a pair of NFL titles in the late fifties, but who had been fired when the team fell back several years later. Ewbank, too, wanted the game very badly.

The Jets won the toss, and on the third play of the game showed the Colts that they meant business when fullback Snell ran head-on into safetyman Volk and sent him to the sidelines. But the Colts forced the New Yorkers to punt and took the ball at their own 27-yard line. And when they got it, they began to move with such ease that the I-told-you-so's were heard everywhere.

A screen pass to Mackey gained 19. Matte ran for 10. Three more running plays got still another first down, and then a pass to tight end Tom Mitchell gained another first and also gave the Colts the ball at the Jets' 19. But suddenly the New York defense toughened. A dropped pass by Richardson didn't help, either, and a sack of Morrall pushed the Colts back farther. Finally,

Lou Michaels missed a 27-yard field-goal try. The Jets had held and the first psychological advantage was theirs.

Early in the game, the Colts defense was also stopping Namath and the Jets, but it was already obvious that the New Yorkers could play on the same field with Baltimore. The Colts coach, Don Shula, had reportedly told his team, "Don't wait for them to lose it. We've got to go out there and win it ourselves." And the Colts seemed to take his advice when they recovered a Jets' fumble late in the quarter at the New York 12.

It was the first big break of the game and most fans figured the Colts would take it in. But after two running plays gained just six yards, quarterback Morrall dropped back and threw over the middle. The ball was tipped, bounced off Tom Mitchell's shoulder, and floated toward the end zone where Jets' cornerback Randy Beverly made a diving interception.

Once again Colts fans were stunned to silence. Who are these guys? they must have thought. And with the ball at the 20, Joe Namath came back out and went to work. This time he decided to go right at the heart of the Baltimore defense. If the Jets could show superiority on the line, they would have a tremendous psychological advantage.

The strategy worked. On four consecutive plays, Namath gave the ball to fullback Snell, who followed mammoth tackle Winston Hill into the right side of the Baltimore defense. The tactic netted 26 yards and a first down at the 46. A short pass to Billy Mathis brought the ball into Colt territory for the first time.

Totally in control of the game, New York Jets' quarterback Joe Namath gives the ball to running back Bill Mathis during the Jets' 16–7 upset of the Baltimore Colts in Super Bowl III. (AP/Wide World Photo)

Mixing his plays extremely well, Namath then went to wide receiver George Sauer for gains of 14 and 11 yards. After a short run by Boozer, Broadway Joe tossed a screen pass to Snell that netted 12 yards all the way to the Baltimore nine. Now it was the underdog New Yorkers who were threatening to score.

Namath still didn't want to be cute. A master strategist, he wanted this score to really mean something. He wanted to show the Colts they were in a war. So he gave the ball to Snell once again. The big fullback bulled his way to the four, then ran in behind Winston

Hill on the next play, scoring as he steamrolled right over middle linebacker Dennis Gaubatz. Jim Turner's conversion made it a 7–0 game, but the score meant much more than that.

The Jets had driven 80 yards, going right at the Colts and taking the yardage in short, tough chunks. In a way, it was almost like a Vince Lombardi–Green Bay Packer drive, intended to show the opposition that the football could be run right down their throats.

It was already early in the second period when the Jets scored, and the Colts must have felt they had to come back fast. A 58-yard run by halfback Matte set them up by putting the ball at the Jets' 16. But when Morrall tried to throw again for the score, Johnny Sample was there to wrest the ball away from Willie Richardson. The former Colt gloated over his interception and the millions of fans watching the game began wondering if they weren't about to witness a historic upset.

Shortly before the half, the Colts tried a trick play, a flea flicker, where Morrall gave the ball to halfback Matte, who faked a run, then flipped the ball back to the quarterback. But when Morrall looked downfield, he didn't see a wide open Jimmy Orr in the end zone. Instead, he threw in the direction of Jerry Hill and the ball was intercepted by Jim Hudson. Once again the Colts' hopes crashed, and the Jets took a 7–0 lead into the locker room at the half.

Shula berated his struggling team, trying to wake them up.

"We're making stupid mistakes," he railed. "We're

stopping ourselves. And you've got them believing that they're better than we are."

The Colts came out looking for a quick score to even the game, but on the first play from scrimmage, Matte fumbled and Jets' linebacker Ralph Baker recovered at the Baltimore 33. Five plays later Jim Turner booted a 32-yard field goal and the Jets had a 10–0 lead.

"Ten points are a lot better than seven," Weeb Ewbank would say. Now his team had a little cushion. Minutes later, another Turner field goal, this one from the 30, padded the lead to 13–0. The Colts were getting desperate. Shula yanked Morrall and sent in Unitas, who was only 80 percent recovered from an arm injury. But Johnny U. had been such a great quarterback for more than a decade that the Colts were hoping he could work his magic one more time.

Only this time it was the Jets' defense that was magical. Unitas fared little better than Morrall, and early in the final period Namath led the Jets on still another drive that resulted in a nine-yard Turner field goal. That gave the Jets a 16–0 lead, and now the Colts were really hard-pressed to avoid the humiliation that would go with being the first NFL team to lose a Super Bowl to the AFL.

Unitas tried valiantly. With less than four minutes remaining he finally got the Colts on the board, full-back Hill scoring from the one. Lou Michaels's kick made it 16–7, but that was as far as the Colts could go. The game ended with that same score. The Jets had done it!

Namath had completed 17 of 28 passes for 206 yards,

eight of them going to George Sauer, while fullback Snell set a Super Bowl mark with 121 rushing yards on 30 carries. But it was the defense that deserved credit for stopping the Colts, and the secondary had made four interceptions. It had been a real team effort.

"Our offensive line won the game with their straight-ahead blocking," crowed Matt Snell.

"It was our defense that broke their backs," Emerson Boozer countered.

In truth, it was a combination of everything. And it was also a quarterback named Joe Namath, who had guaranteed a victory and had delivered. His play-calling had kept the Colts off balance all afternoon, and his flawless execution left no room for mistakes. Even the Colts had to admit that Joe delivered, had kept his promise. He had engineered probably the greatest football upset of all time, one that is still talked about to this day.

And after it was over, reporters had all kinds of questions, many of which centered on Namath's guaranteeing a victory and thus putting all kinds of pressure on himself.

But Joe just smiled and said, "A guy who doesn't have confidence just doesn't come from a good family."

Upsets in the Ring

The sport of boxing has often been the subject of controversy over the years. In fact, it is the very nature of the sport itself that has often spawned vigorous debate. Should a sport where two men are trying to knock one another out really be allowed? But despite its detractors, the sport has survived around the world for literally hundreds of years.

And in that time there have been many great champions, ring artists who are the equal of the finest athletes in the other sports. The list is a long one, but even the casual fight fan will recognize names like Jack Dempsey, Joe Louis, Rocky Marciano, Sugar Ray Robinson, Floyd Patterson, Roberto Duran, and Marvelous Marvin Hagler.

There are others, of course, but these are just some of the great ones who have helped forge the history of the sport. And while there certainly have been a number of outstanding boxers in the past 20 years, there have really been two fighters who have captured the imagination of the public both in and out of the ring. And while these two men were both very great champions in their own right, they have also been involved in two of the very greatest upsets in the history of the sport.

The two fighters are Muhammad Ali and Sugar Ray Leonard.

Though Ali was a heavyweight, and Leonard a welterweight and later a middleweight, in many ways the two were cut from the same mold. Both were extremely fast of hand and foot. They could bedazzle their opponents with fancy footwork, outspeed them with a quick left jab and lightning-quick combinations, or, if the occasion called for it, unleash knockout power.

And to top it off, both were consummate showmen, giving fans their money's worth whenever they'd step in the ring during their primes. Both fighters began by winning a gold medal for their country at the Olympic Games. But then their careers took very diverse paths, only to link up once again whenever fans talk about great boxing upsets. Both men won a key fight in their careers, a fight in which they were clearly the underdog, a fight nearly everyone said they couldn't win.

For Muhammad Ali, the first moment of glory came at the 1960 Olympics in Rome, Italy. His name was Cassius Clay then, and he was an 18-year-old light-heavyweight who danced and jabbed his way to Olympic Gold, easily defeating older and more experienced fighters. Young Cassius told the press that the gold medal was the greatest thrill of his life and that he was going to sleep with it around his neck.

In October following the Olympics, Cassius Clay turned professional, and as a heavyweight he began his career by defeating a journeyman named Tunny Hunsaker. In the following 15 months, the youngster won 10 straight fights, most of them taking place in his hometown of Louisville, Kentucky, or in Miami.

By February of 1962, Cassius Clay was a bona fide heavyweight and fighting the main event at Madison Square Garden in New York City. That night he knocked out a solid heavyweight named Sonny Banks in just four rounds, and before long he began trumpeting his own cause, proclaiming himself "the greatest," and telling people he would become the next heavyweight champion of the world.

Not many people believed him then. They figured he was just another kid who liked to hear himself talk. But by February of 1964, the undefeated Clay was ready for a title fight. He would be challenging the then heavyweight champ, Charles "Sonny" Liston, who had taken the title by knocking out Floyd Patterson in just one round. And in their rematch, Liston did it again, dispatching the popular Patterson in one. A burly man with power in both hands, Liston's baleful stare was enough to frighten most men. And in the ring he looked unbeatable.

Yet it was Clay who was predicting victory, and he

surprised the boxing world when he danced and jabbed his way to the title. An overconfident and perhaps out-of-shape Liston just couldn't cope with the youngster's speed and refused to come out to answer the bell for the seventh round. Clay had done it. At age 22, he was heavyweight champion of the world!

With the world at his feet, the new champion suddenly made an announcement that surprised many. He said he had become a Black Muslim, a group that followed the religion of Islam, and in the 1960s stood for a separate black society apart from whites. He also said that he was discarding the name Cassius Clay, which he said was his slave name, and would now be known as Muhammad Ali.

Because the 1960s were a time of political and social change in the United States, many people distrusted the Black Muslims. They thought the group was militant and dangerous, though the Muslims said they worried only about self-defense, protecting their own. Nevertheless, by joining the group Muhammad Ali lost a great deal of the popularity he had gained among the general public.

As a fighter, however, he was getting better all the time. In a return bout he knocked out Liston in one round, then fought and defeated former champ Floyd Patterson, taunting the popular Patterson for 12 torturous rounds before the fight was stopped. To many, Muhammad Ali had become a villain, and they wanted to see him beaten in the ring.

But that wasn't about to happen. He had perhaps the greatest foot speed of any heavyweight who ever lived, and made the boxing ring his own personal stage. On his bicycle, no one could catch him, and when he came down, he would land combinations in bunches. While he didn't have a single, big knockout punch, he was nevertheless a very dangerous fighter and a beautiful one to watch.

He had grown to a 6′3″, 220-pounder, yet he moved with the speed and grace of a much lighter man. He could stop and change direction in an instant. Instead of blocking punches with his hands and arms, he would sometimes let his arms dangle at his sides and just dance away, or pull his head back at such an angle that the punch would just miss him. He was the only fighter around with the speed and reflexes to get away with such unconventional ring behavior.

By 1967 he had defended his title nine times, winning easily in every bout. The Vietnam War was raging at that time, and toward the end of the year word came that Muhammad Ali was about to be drafted into the army. To the surprise of no one, he refused induction, stating he was a minister of the Muslim faith and should be exempt.

Upon his refusal he was placed under arrest and the boxing people quickly moved by stripping him of the heavyweight title. Ali never went to jail. He continued to appeal his case and it was finally dismissed. But during that three-year period he was kept out of the ring. They were what should have been his peak years, years in which he would have improved his ring skills even more.

In October of 1970, Ali was finally given a license to

fight again. He was 28 years old and rusty. The question was, could he again become the great fighter he once had been? His comeback fight was against a good heavyweight, Jerry Quarry, and he stopped Quarry in three rounds.

Five months later, on March 8, 1971, Ali found himself fighting for the title again, this time against unbeaten Joe Frazier, who had become champ during Ali's exile. Frazier was a straight-ahead brawler who wore opponents down. He was also a power puncher with a devastating left hook. It certainly wouldn't be an easy fight for the former champ.

It turned out to be a grueling fight, 15 rounds of nonstop action. And it was close all the way. In the 14th, Frazier knocked Ali down with a big left hook. For a split second it looked over. But Muhammad got up and finished the round and the fight. However, the knockdown helped Frazier win a unanimous decision, giving Ali the first defeat of his career.

But the ex-champ didn't quit. In fact, after the Frazier fight, Muhammad Ali once again began winning over his former fans. No longer were the Black Muslims feared as a militant group, and while he remained a member, Ali moved back into the mainstream, appearing frequently on television talk shows and in public, where his magnetic personality again prevailed. And he kept promising he would regain his title.

In March of 1973 he lost his second fight, a tough battle with Ken Norton in which his jaw was broken. By now it was obvious that Muhammad Ali was no longer the same fighter he had been. Much of his foot speed was gone and he couldn't escape punches as easily as he had before. The three-year layoff had undoubtedly taken its toll.

But in September, he fought Norton again and this time won a close decision. By that time there was a new heavyweight champ. Hard-punching George Foreman had knocked out Frazier to win the crown. Now Muhammad Ali wanted to fight Foreman. Before that, he went up against Frazier again and this time won a tough, 12-round decision. Then he signed to meet Foreman for the title, the fight to be held in October of 1974 in the African nation of Zaire.

It was a fight most people felt Ali could not win. He was 32 years old, past his prime, and going against an extremely strong and hard-punching champion. Even the so-called experts figured he was in for a very tough night.

"I don't care what the scorecards say," commented Eddie Futch, the manager of Joe Frazier, "because Ali has to be erect after 15 for the scorecards to count, and there is no way he will be. He isn't strong enough. Strength on strength, he can't handle George."

Dick Sadler, Foreman's manager, was also extremely confident. "When George hits a guy, he lifts him off his feet. To win, Ali must have some sort of a break, a fluke. There's too much against him."

That seemed to be the consensus. Ali just couldn't win. Yet Ali kept telling anyone who'd listen that he was still the greatest and that he would win. It seemed that only his manager, Angelo Dundee, agreed.

"My guy will knock him out midway in the fight," Dundee said. But very few listened.

Only Floyd Patterson among the heavyweights had ever lost then regained the title. Muhammad Ali wanted to be the second to do it, and on fight night, most people watching thought he would try to do it by jabbing and moving, dancing to avoid Foreman's powerful blows. But once again Muhammad Ali fooled them all.

When the bell sounded for round one, Ali came out and immediately retreated into a corner, covering up with his hands and arms. No one could believe it. Even the men in his corner were yelling for him to move. Maybe he was so fearful of Foreman's power that he was frozen? But when he moved out of the corner, he settled immediately on the ropes, with Foreman throwing punches at him.

Ali was picking off the punches with his arms and shoulders, and also leaning back out of the way. Right at the end of the round he suddenly came off the ropes and caught the champ with several quick sharp punches in the face. Foreman seemed puzzled, as well as angry.

With Dundee and the other cornermen still telling him to move and jab, Ali continued to ignore their instructions. "I know what I'm doing," was all he would say, and he continued to lie on the ropes.

Foreman kept throwing punches, but very few were getting through. Late in round three, Ali again came off the ropes to catch Foreman with a quick combination. Some thought the champ's knees buckled slightly. If there was a question about Foreman, it involved his stamina. He was such a devastating puncher that most of his fights ended very quickly, and he was never tested over the long haul.

In the fourth, Ali began taunting the champ, telling him he wasn't hurt, that his punches were doing no damage. Foreman got even madder and punched more. Before long, his punches began to lose their snap, and they were coming in much slower. Suddenly everyone knew what Muhammad Ali was doing. Foreman was tiring badly. Ali's strategy, which he would later refer to as the "Rope-a-Dope," was working.

Ali began connecting with more quick combinations, and finally toward the middle of the fight, ringsiders heard him sound an ominous warning to Foreman.

"Now it's my turn," he told the champ.

With that, Ali became the aggressor, peppering Foreman with sharp combinations and right-hand leads. By the eighth round, the champ was wobbly. His legs weren't working, and Ali jumped to the advantage, flooring Foreman with a combination of lefts and rights. The champ tried to get up, but he didn't make it. The fight was over. Muhammad Ali had done it, and just the way Angelo Dundee called it. He had stopped George Foreman in the eighth round to regain the heavyweight title in one of sports' greatest upsets.

It wasn't the end of Muhammad Ali's great career. In fact, he would later lose the title to Leon Spinks and come back to regain it a third time. But in spite of all his great fights, the one against George Foreman will

A determined Muhammad Ali bounces a left jab off champion George Foreman's chin in their 1974 heavy-weight-title fight. Ali shocked the boxing world by regaining the crown from the heavily favored Foreman. (AP/Wide World Photo)

always be remembered as the time Ali beat the odds and defied all logic. He pulled off one of the great upsets ever—unless, of course, you asked him. His answer probably would be . . . What upset? I always told you I was the greatest.

Two years after Muhammad Ali pulled off his great upset in 1974, another set of boxing heroes came on the scene. They were the men who comprised the 1976 United States Olympic boxing team. U.S. fighters tra-ditionally did not do well in Olympic competition because the European and Cuban fighters were older and had more experience. But in 1976 the American team was so outstanding that they garnered five gold medals.

The gold medal winners were Leo Randolph; the brothers Spinks, Leon and Michael; Howard Davis, voted the outstanding boxer in the Olympics; and Ray Charles Leonard, known in ring circles as Sugar Ray.

Of all the 1976 Olympians, Sugar Ray was perhaps the most charismatic. Possessed of a bright personality and quick smile, he was both charming and intelligent. In the ring he was an artist, not unlike Muhammad Ali. He was swift of both feet and hands, could stick and move like a boxer, as well as play to the crowd with antics that were sometimes called showboating. But it was part of his overall ring presence.

But Leonard had something else going for him. In addition to his boxing skills, he had a fighter's heart. When it came to crunch time, he was right there. And if it meant digging down deep for that little extra and slugging it out with an opponent in order to win, Ray Leonard would do it.

To take the gold medal, Sugar Ray had to defeat a tough Cuban fighter named Andras Aldama, a light-welterweight with a tremendous knockout punch. And Leonard had two very swollen, sore hands from his earlier fights. But he knew this one was for everything.

"One more fight, then it's over," he said. "I've been fighting here with one hand. Now I'll let go with everything. What do I have to lose?"

And that's what he did. Using his great foot speed to circle away from Aldama's big left, he punched in flurries and dropped the Cuban just before the end of the second round. Then in the third and final round he let it all out, putting together a furious three minutes that left Aldama holding on as the bell sounded. Sugar Ray won the gold medal by a 5–0 decision.

After the Olympics, Ray Leonard said he would fight no more. He talked about returning to school. But it wasn't long before he changed his mind, citing that professional boxing would give him a chance to do some things for his family. Under the guidance of Angelo Dundee, the same man who had helped shape Muhammad Ali's ring career, Sugar Ray began his pro career.

Once again he began dazzling opponents with his combination of speed and power, and his ability to finish fast. He also gained experience and continued to improve, as well as becoming a top attraction by virtue of his style and personality. Those guiding his career didn't rush him, and by the time he fought the tough Wildredo Benitez for the welterweight title in November of 1979 he was ready.

Sugar Ray won the fight and his first title. It was a hard-fought battle and the first of several epic ring wars in which he would engage. In 1980 he suffered the first and only loss of his career when the great lightweight champion, Roberto Duran, moved up to the welterweight class and decisioned Sugar Ray in a very close bout.

Ray had taken up the challenge and fought Duran's fight, a close-in brawl in which he abandoned much of his movement and ring generalship. But in a return

Intensity is written all over Sugar Ray Leonard's face as he sets out to capture the middleweight title from the champ, Marvelous Marvin Hagler. (Courtesy Home Box Office)

bout the same year, he thoroughly confused and frustrated Duran with his speed and hit-and-run tactics. So frustrated by his inability to catch Sugar Ray was Duran that he actually quit in the sixth round, just turning his back and saying *"no mas,"* which in Spanish means "no more."

So Sugar Ray was the champion once again. He would soon take the junior middleweight crown from Ayub Kulule, then fight another classic against Thomas "Hit Man" Hearns to unify the welterweight title. It was a bout in which Leonard was actually trailing on points in the 14th round when he summoned up his great reserve once again and stopped Hearns on a technical knockout. He was now being called one of the greatest of all time, and sometimes even being compared with his namesake, Sugar Ray Robinson.

But then, without warning, things changed. Soon after a bout with a journeyman fighter named Bruce Finch, Sugar Ray learned he had a detached retina in his eye and would need surgery. The operation was termed a success and there was now talk about a big-money fight with middleweight champion Marvelous Marvin Hagler. But Sugar Ray again surprised the boxing world by announcing his retirement. He had already made a great deal of money and said he did not want to risk permanent eye damage, perhaps even blindness, by continuing his career.

So it seemed that the boxing world had seen the last of Sugar Ray Leonard. Of course, there were those who said he would get the urge again and try a come-back. He did, some two years later. In May of 1984 he came out of retirement to fight a journeyman named Kevin Howard. Sugar Ray did not look good. He was knocked down once, but got up to stop Howard in the late rounds.

Then, right after the fight, he shocked everyone by announcing his retirement once again, saying he just didn't feel as if he wanted to continue. Now, he would surely never fight again. Or so it seemed.

For the next several years he seemed content with endorsements, public appearances, and doing fight commentary on television. He remained a popular and sought-after personality. And during this time, the fame and legend of Marvelous Marvin Hagler grew. The undisputed middleweight champ was defeating all comers and garnering a reputation as the best fighter, pound for pound, in the world.

Every now and then, rumors would surface that Sugar Ray would again come out of retirement. And Ray himself said that the only fight that could draw him out would be with Hagler. But as time passed, a Leonard-Hagler fight seemed more and more unlikely. Fighters just don't come back, at least not successfully, after a layoff of several years. That's too much to ask of any fighter, even a great one like Sugar Ray.

But amazingly, the fight was made. It was set for April of 1987 at Caesar's Palace in Las Vegas. Though Ray would earn about $12 million for the fight, he said it was neither the money nor the championship that he was after.

"It's Hagler. I just want to beat him," he said. "He's the only man in the world who could make me come out of retirement and fight."

The ultimate challenge. To those who really knew Ray best, it seemed a legitimate reason. But almost all the experts, including his friends, didn't think Sugar Ray had a chance. In fact, many of them feared for his safety.

Hagler, after all, was the best, a fighter who took years to win the respect of the general public, not to mention the huge purses that were offered to others. He looked at each new fight as a personal war, and his motto for each was "destruct and destroy." He gave no quarter and came into each bout in tiptop physical shape. In recent years he had won epic battles with Thomas Hearns and John Mugabi. In fact, coming in to the Leonard fight, Hagler had defended his middleweight title 12 straight times, and had not lost a single fight in 11 years.

Talk about being an underdog. With the exception of the Howard fight in 1984, Sugar Ray had not fought in five years and nearly two months. There was no way he could regain his former skills in time to challenge a great fighter like Hagler. True, the Marvelous one was in his thirties now and undoubtedly beginning to slide back, but Sugar was also past 30 and was not even taking a tune-up fight before stepping into the ring with Hagler. The same question kept arising again and again. How could he possibly win?

Interest in the bout was enormous. Once again Sugar Ray would be on center stage, and to some, this was the real reason he was fighting, the reason Muhammad Ali toiled for so long. Fighters get used to that limelight and don't like to give it up.

But as fight time approached, Hagler continued to be the heavy favorite. The word was that Leonard wasn't even looking that good in training camp. He showed some flashes of the old Sugar Ray, but not that many. There were a few who went out on a limb and said that Leonard's style would frustrate Hagler, but only if he could keep his legs over the 12-round distance. But Leonard backers were few and far between. His main supporter, however, was trainer Angelo Dundee, the same man who had predicted Ali's upset victory over George Foreman some 13 years earlier.

"My guy is going to outbox him and outthink him," Dundee said. "He's not even supposed to be fighting,

Once again showing the skills that made him a great champion, Leonard connects with a left hook as Hagler tries to cover up. (Courtesy Home Box Office)

but that's what gets you juiced up. This has never been done before. We're rewriting the boxing record book. Believe me, Ray Leonard can't lose."

It was a bold prediction, but once the fight began, it was obvious that Sugar Ray was not going to pull an Ali and try some strategy no one expected. He was Sugar Ray, dancing and moving, and making Hagler miss. He was also spotting his punches, swatting Hagler with a jab, then connecting with an uppercut. And toward the end of the round he fired a salvo of punches, a Sugar Ray flurry of old.

He was also entertaining in his old way, mocking Hagler, daring the champ to hit him while he mugged for the crowd. Using this style and still operating on fresh legs, Sugar took the early rounds, piling up a big

91

point lead in the first six rounds. But by the sixth, it appeared to many that he was beginning to slow down a bit and that Hagler was also starting to find the range.

In the seventh round, Hagler caught Leonard with a big left hook, rocking the challenger and sending him to the ropes. The Marvelous one was all over Ray, firing punches and trying to put his longtime nemesis on the canvas. But Ray withstood the barrage and finished the round. In spite of his big lead in points, the question now was could he finish the fight?

In the next round Hagler was hoping to make the fight a brawl. Ringsiders heard him say to Sugar Ray, "Come on, slug!" But Leonard's answer was a quick, "No chance."

During the next couple of rounds Hagler repeatedly tried to pin Ray against the ropes. And on the occasions when he did, Sugar was able to reach down deep inside himself to return Hagler's punches with flurries of his own, enabling him to get off the ropes and back into the center of the ring. Whether it was Sugar Ray's style, or Hagler's advancing age, or a combination of both, the champion just couldn't put together enough heavy punches to put Sugar Ray away.

In the 12th and final round, Ray was obviously tired, but once again his great will to win was in evidence as he fought in flurries and kept Hagler from mounting any kind of sustained attack. Now everyone waited anxiously for the decision.

The announcement made boxing history. Sugar Ray Leonard had won a split decision. He was the new

At the final bell, Sugar Ray seems to sense that he has pulled off one of the most monumental upsets in boxing history. (Courtesy Home Box Office)

middleweight champion of the world. But more importantly, he had defied logic and the hard lessons of boxing to pull off one of the greatest upsets in the history of any sport. Very few people thought he had a chance to win, but he had.

"I was never interested in the title, just in beating Hagler," Sugar Ray said, after the fight. "My strategy was stick and move, hit and run, taunt and frustrate. I knew it would be a tough fight, but I beat him to the punch."

Hagler, of course, didn't agree with the decision. He thought he had won the fight and wanted a rematch. But true to his character, Sugar Ray Leonard promptly retired once again, leaving people to guess whether he would make still another comeback in the future.

Whether Sugar Ray Leonard fights again or not doesn't really matter. The Hagler fight is in the books forever. And perhaps the real significance of the bout can be captured in a quick bit of dialogue between Sugar Ray and his manager, Mike Trainer, shortly after the fight ended.

"You know, I don't really realize what I just did," Ray said.

"Don't worry about it," Trainer answered, "the rest of the world does."

The Wildcats' Surprise Crown

The NCAA basketball tournament has become one of the great spectacles in all of sport. With the best college teams in the country all vying for a spot in the Final Four and an eventual national championship, cage fans have come to expect exciting and nail-biting basketball.

There have been a number of dominant teams since the tournament began in 1939. There were Adolph Rupp's great Kentucky ballclubs of the late 1940s, with Alex Groza and Ralph Beard; the Bill Russell–led San Francisco teams that won a pair of titles in 1955 and '56, the Cincinnati Bearcat club of the early 1960s that reached the final three straight years, and finally UCLA.

That was the greatest college dynasty ever. Guided by the veteran coach John Wooden, the Bruins won 10

NCAA titles in 12 years beginning in 1964. Along the way, the club had a pair of dominant centers, first Lew Alcindor (later known as Kareem Abdul-Jabbar) and then Bill Walton, with a supporting cast of outstanding players, including several other all-Americans.

The last Bruin title came in 1975, and no team has been able to win back-to-back titles since the UCLA teams of 1972 and '73. With the tournament becoming more competitive, and with more teams being allowed to participate, repeating has become very difficult.

But so have real upsets. There are so many fine college basketball teams today that it would be extremely difficult for a Cinderella team to work its way to the Final Four, let alone win. But it has happened, though never in quite the same way as it did in 1985. For that was not only a year that a Cinderella team provided perhaps the most dramatic and unexpected upset in NCAA history, but also a year in which a team with a truly dominant center was attempting to become the first team to repeat as national champions since the great UCLA teams of 1972 and 1973.

The team trying to repeat was Georgetown. The Hoyas under Coach John Thompson were always a hustling, pressing ballclub that never quit and could hurt you in many different ways. Then, in 1981–82, Georgetown added freshman center Patrick Ewing, an aggressive seven-footer, and the team became a national power.

In Ewing's freshman year, the Hoyas went all the way to the NCAA finals before losing to North Carolina by a single point, 63–62. Two years later they were back, and this time they became national champions with an 84–75 victory over the University of Houston. And in 1985, Ewing's senior year, Georgetown returned to the Final Four for the third time in four seasons, and the Hoyas wanted a second national championshp very badly.

Oddly enough, the teams they had to fear the most came from their own conference. Over the past decade, the Big East had become one of the most powerful and competitive conferences in the country. Besides Georgetown, St. John's, Syracuse, Boston College, and Villanova had fine teams. In fact, St. John's had beaten Georgetown during the regular season and was the number-one-ranked team in the country for several weeks.

Though Georgetown had won the Big East Tournament after the regular season, the other aforementioned Big East teams also received NCAA tournament bids. The one surprise was Villanova, which was coming into the tournament with just a 19–10 record. That's not bad, but teams with 10 losses don't usually get bids, especially when there are a number of other teams within their conference with better marks.

But the Wildcats, led by their dynamic and emotional coach, Rollie Massimino, always played an exciting brand of basketball and, despite their losses, had some fine individual talent. Still, the selection was questionable, especially after the Wildcats dropped their final regular-season game of the year to unheralded Pittsburgh by 23 points.

Yet once the tournament started, the Wildcats

This is what an NCAA championship team looks like. Back row, left to right: Wyatt Maker, Ed Pinckney, Mark Plansky, Harold Pressley, Coach Rollie Massimino, Dwayne McClain, Connally Brown, and Chuck Everson. Front row, left to right: Dwight Wilbur, Veltra Dawson, R. C. Massimino, Gary McLain, Brian Harrington, Harold Jensen, and Steve Pinone. (Courtesy Villanova University)

seemed to be a different team. Massimino had his club primed and ready. With nothing to lose because they weren't expected to win, the Wildcats began playing outstanding basketball.

Led by point guard Gary McLain, shooting guard Harold Jensen, center Ed Pinckney, and forwards Dwayne McClain and Harold Pressley, the Wildcats won their regional and found themselves an unlikely entry in the Final Four.

Joining Massimino's crew were two other Big East teams, Georgetown as expected, and St. John's, along with Memphis State. The Hoyas were installed as heavy favorites to repeat, while Villanova was considered the least likely to win it all. In the semifinals, Georgetown dispensed of rival St. John's, winning by a big, 77–59 count.

Villanova, in the meantime, had to play Memphis State, led by 6'10" all-America Keith Lee, and seven-foot William Bedford. Add to those two point guard André Turner, and it was felt the Tigers had too much height and firepower for the Wildcats.

But the large crowd at the Adolph Rupp Arena in Lexington, Kentucky, couldn't believe it as Massimino's troops took the court and then took the game away from Memphis State, 52–45. Asked about being beaten by a Cinderella team, Memphis State's Dana Kirk quipped, "If Villanova is Cinderella, then Cinderella wears boots."

To most people, the final game would be a mere formality. Georgetown would just have to take the court, go through the motions, and 40 minutes later emerge as national champs for the second straight year. One local newspaperman jokingly suggested that the NCAA not even bother to hold the final game.

As for Coach Massimino, he knew what his ballclub was up against. "We're going to have to play a perfect game to win," he said, "and not even that may be enough. We can't afford to turn the ball over too much against their various pressure defenses, and we're going to have to shoot in the 50 percent range."

It was no secret what Georgetown would do. They would pressure and defense you to death. The Hoyas had been holding their opponents to about 40 percent shooting from the floor, so Massimino was asking a great deal of his team. Offensively, Georgetown supported Ewing in the middle with the outside shooting of Reggie Williams and David Wingate. Michael Jackson was a fine point guard, while Bill Martin gave the big guy rebounding support underneath.

Georgetown also wanted that early lead so they could continue to force the pace of the game. Slowdown wasn't their style, and Massimino knew it. If there was a practical way to slow things down, he would.

But in the early going it began looking like a typical Georgetown game. With Reggie Williams hitting from the outside, the Hoyas forged to a 20–14 lead. To most observers, it looked as if the rout was on.

Only the Wildcats didn't see it that way. They refused to wilt under the relentless Georgetown pressure. In fact, guard Gary McLain was breaking the Hoya press and trap with some brilliant ball handling. And after he got the ball over half court he would slow things up and try to set up for the good shot.

"Even though Georgetown had that 20–14 lead early," said one reporter, "you could see Villanova hadn't panicked. They were playing under control and had hit on seven of their first eight shots for their 14 points."

They were also forcing Georgetown outside with a tight matchup zone. And while the Hoyas were taking more shots, they just weren't falling, especially after Thompson pulled Williams from the game for a rest.

Slowly, the Wildcats fought back and closed the gap. The sellout house at Rupp Arena couldn't believe how the Wildcats were hanging in there. In fact, when the buzzer sounded to end the first half, Villanova was sitting on a one-point lead at 29–28. It was a ballgame, all right.

Coming out with renewed confidence after intermission, the Wildcats extended their lead to 36–30 and, despite the relentless Georgetown pressure, still held the lead at 53–48. The Hoyas continued to get more shots, but the Wildcats weren't missing, and they were also getting more time at the foul line as the aggressive Hoya defense was causing the refs to blow their whistles.

But the Hoyas weren't about to quit. Suddenly their pressure caused a number of turnovers and Georgetown was quick to take advantage. A six-point run gave them the lead for the first time in the second half, 54–53. Once again the millions of fans watching in person and on TV thought the Hoyas had finally worn Villanova down, that they would pull away. Thinking his team might be losing its momentum, Massimino called a time-out.

"I told them to settle down and just run a play," he said later. "I also reminded them that Georgetown was a great team and was going to make a run sooner or later. And then I told them once again that we were going to win the game."

Fewer than five minutes remained now. Villanova tried to get back in it, but when Ewing stripped Pinckney of the ball, it marked three straight posses-

A jubilant Rollie Massimino celebrates with players Ed Pinckney (54) and Dwayne McClain just moments after coaching Villanova to the NCAA title in an upset victory over Georgetown in 1985. (Courtesy Villanova University)

sions that the Wildcats had failed to score. A Georgetown hoop now and Villanova would really be in a hole.

But suddenly the Wildcats got a break. Bill Martin's pass bounced off the foot of Horace Broadnax and Villanova got the ball back. The Cats worked to set up a play. Finally, they threw the ball to Harold Jensen on the right side. He took a quick jumper. Swish! Villanova had regained the lead at 55–54 with just 2:36 to play!

With just 2:11 left, Pinckney calmly sank a pair of free throws. They would be the first 2 of 11 Villanova free throws down the stretch as Georgetown desperately tried to get the ball and avoid an incredible upset loss. But every time it looked as if the Hoyas would get the lead, the Wildcats would hit again from the charity stripe. The Hoyas just couldn't make it this time, and Villanova's cool prevailed as they won the game, 66–64, and the national championship.

It was an incredible victory. To win it, Villanova had shot 78.6 percent from the field, including an unreal 90 percent in the second half alone. They sank 22 of their 28 field-goal attempts. By contrast, Georgetown hit on 29 of 53 shots, but the Wildcats also had an enormous advantage on the foul line, hitting 22 of 27 as compared with just 6 of 8 for the Hoyas.

Dwayne McClain led Villanova with 17 points, while Pinckney had 16 and Jensen 14. Gary McLain had played the entire 40 minutes at point guard and committed just a pair of turnovers despite constant pressure and harassment from the Georgetown defense. It had been an incredible victory, an upset of huge proportions.

Pinckney was named the tournament's Most Valuable Player, while a disbelieving Patrick Ewing told the press, "I still think we're number one."

But number one on this day was Rollie Massimino and his Villanova Wildcats. They had done what all the experts said they couldn't do, and they had done it with style. As Gary McLain said afterward:

"I knew the classy program was going to win the championship. And we're very classy."

Mets Magic, Circa 1969

Can an expansion baseball team that never finished higher than ninth place suddenly win a pennant and play for a world championship? Sounds impossible, doesn't it? But it really happened, and even today it's looked upon as something of a miracle, a major sports upset that will never be forgotten.

The team was the New York Mets. But not the Mets of Dwight Gooden, Ron Darling, Keith Hernandez, Darryl Strawberry, and Gary Carter. No, these were the Mets of Tom Seaver, Jerry Koosman, Cleon Jones, Ron Swoboda, and Tommie Agee. A different team; a different era. They were the Mets who, in 1969, shocked the entire baseball world.

New York was always a hotbed of baseball. The Big Apple played host to the perennial world champions, the New York Yankees, as well as a pair of National

League teams, the New York Giants and Brooklyn Dodgers. The rivalries were great, the legends plentiful. Even in the 1950s the argument raged. Which team had the best centerfielder? Was it Mickey Mantle of the Yanks, Willie Mays of the Giants, or Duke Snider of the Dodgers?

And there were plenty of so-called subway series. The Yanks and Dodgers met in the World Series in 1941, 1947, 1949, 1952 and '53, and again in 1955, while the Yanks collided with the Giants in 1951.

But suddenly, after the 1957 season, it all came to an end. Though no one believed it would actually happen, both the Dodgers and Giants moved out of New York, the Dodgers to Los Angeles and the Giants to San Francisco. At the beginning of the 1958 season, New York just had a single major-league baseball team, the Yankees.

It stayed that way for just four years. For in 1962, a new team came to New York. Christened the New York Metropolitans, Mets for short, the new ballclub was initially made up of over-the-hill veterans, untried youngsters, and a lot of mediocrity. The team's first superstar was its manager, the venerable and beloved Casey Stengel, who had once piloted the Yanks to a brace of world championships in the late 1940s and early 1950s.

The "Ol' Perfesser," as he was called, entertained the fans and media with his own brand of humor and manner of speech, affectionately called "Stengelese." Yet while all this was happening, the Mets were losing, and losing big. In their first season they dropped 120

105

games, and it didn't get much better as the years passed. The team quickly became the laughingstock of the entire National League.

On more than one occasion, Stengel was heard to plead, "Can't anyone here play this game?" But for four straight seasons the Mets were dead last. Finally, after the 1965 season Stengel retired and Wes Westrum became the new manager. The Mets responded by climbing out of the basement in 1966, by one notch. They finished ninth.

But the next year they were once again last. Only in 1967 they had discovered a pitcher, a strong-armed rookie righthander named Tom Seaver, who stepped in and won 16 games for the lowly Mets. Besides being a talented young pitcher, Seaver was also a fierce competitor who didn't like to lose. He began spreading this feeling among the other young players on the team.

A year later the team had still another manager. He was Gil Hodges, who had been an outstanding first baseman for the old Brooklyn Dodgers and was still loved in the New York area. He was also a fine manager, having piloted the Washington Senators in the American League and helping to bring about a marked improvement in that team.

When he took over the Mets, Hodges went about building a different kind of team. Seaver was back and would win another 16 games. He was joined in 1968 by a rookie lefthander named Jerry Koosman, who surprised everyone by winning 19 games. With these two young stars leading the way, the Mets got out of the cellar again, finishing ninth in a 10-team league.

The World Champion 1969 New York Mets captured the imagination of the entire baseball world when they upset the Baltimore Orioles in five games. Manager Gil Hodges is in the second row from the bottom, fifth from the left. Star pitchers Tom Seaver and Jerry Koosman are in the third row from the bottom, fifth and sixth from the left, right behind Hodges. (National Baseball Library, Cooperstown, N.Y.)

But there were some other players of promise, as well. Jerry Grote was an outstanding defensive catcher who knew how to handle the growing young pitching staff. Outfielders Cleon Jones, Tommie Agee, and Ron Swoboda all showed power potential at the plate. Ed Kranepool was a young first baseman who often had big things predicted for him. And Bud Harrelson could play shortstop as well as anyone in the league.

At the outset of the 1969 season some experts, citing the good young players, felt the Mets might go up another notch or two in the standings. But no one thought the club had pennant potential as yet. The major leagues had expanded once again, and for the first time there was divisional play, with the two division winners meeting in a playoff series to determine the pennant winner and representative in the World Series.

So this time the Mets would be in a 6-team division instead of a 10-team league. Right from the outset it was obvious the club was no longer a pushover. Seaver and Koosman were joined by another young starter named Gary Gentry, as well as a fireballing righthander with control problems named Nolan Ryan. But when his game was right, he was almost impossible to hit.

The team also made a midseason trade that brought power-hitting Donn Clendenon over from Pittsburgh, and veteran Ed Charles had solidified the infield at third. By midseason the Mets had moved closer to the top and by August were in second place, chasing the front-running Chicago Cubs. The New Yorkers had a well-rounded team, and suddenly they were in contention for a division title. It seemed impossible.

Impossible? Maybe. But someone must have forgotten to tell the 25 guys dressed in New York Mets' uniforms. For in mid-September they whipped the Cubs two straight, then a day later drove into the top spot for the first time in the club's history. Now people were beginning to call the Mets a team of destiny. It seemed that nearly every day there was a new hero, another player rising to the occasion and helping the club to win a ballgame.

During the last weeks of the season it became increasingly obvious that the Mets were about to do the impossible. The team showed no signs of faltering. In fact, if anything, they were getting better. Late in September it became official. The New York Mets were the champions of the Eastern Division of the National League. The club won 38 of its final 48 games to take the division and now prepared to meet the Atlanta Braves, the Western Division winner, in the first-ever best-of-five National League playoff series.

A number of the Mets' players had great seasons. Seaver finished with a 25–7 record and would later win the Cy Young Award as the best pitcher in the league. Koosman, despite some early-season arm problems, wound up at 17–9, while rookie Gentry was a 13-game winner. Leftfielder Jones was near the top of the league with a .340 average, and centerfielder Agee led the team in homers with 26 and RBIs with 76.

In the first-ever National League playoffs, the Mets had to face the Atlanta Braves, a team featuring the great Henry Aaron and a host of hard-hitting players. But it's an old baseball adage that good pitching always stops good hitting. And good pitching was something the Mets had in abundance.

But the surprise was the Mets' hitters. They bombed the Atlanta pitchers for 37 hits and 27 runs in three games and they won them all to take the National League pennant. The fans at New York's Shea Stadium went wild, tearing out huge chunks of turf in one of baseball's craziest celebrations.

Now the Amazin's had one more hurdle to clear. In

the World Series that year they would be facing the Baltimore Orioles, considered by many the best team in baseball. The Orioles had won their division by an incredible 19 games and then had demolished the Minnesota Twins in the American League playoffs, also in three straight.

Baltimore's lineup looked like just a small variation of the American League All-Star team. The O's were led by the Robinsons, outfielder Frank and third baseman Brooks. Both were the best in the league at their positions. First sacker Boog Powell was coming off a super year with 37 homers and 121 RBIs.

Outfielders Paul Blair and Don Buford, as well as infielders Mark Belanger and Davey Johnson, joined the others to give the Orioles a formidable starting lineup. But that wasn't all. Baltimore also had an outstanding pitching staff, led by 20-game winners Mike Cuellar and Dave McNally, as well as Jim Palmer, who won 16. Despite the Mets' Cinderella story, the Orioles were made heavy favorites to win the series.

The 1969 World Series opened at Baltimore's Memorial Stadium with Seaver pitching for the Mets and Cuellar for the Orioles. After the Mets went out in the first, Don Buford stepped in to lead it off for the O's. He took Seaver's first pitch for a ball, then promptly deposited the next one in the right-field stands for a home run!

Baltimore fans went wild. Some team of destiny. Two pitches and their club already had a 1–0 lead. It stayed at 1–0 until the fourth when the usually light-hitting Mark Belanger drove home a run with a single, giving

110

Baltimore a two-run lead. Pitcher Cuellar then singled home still another run, and Buford came up to double home the fourth. So after just four innings, the Orioles had a 4–0 lead against a man considered by many the best pitcher in baseball.

The Mets could never really get started against Cuellar, and the veteran lefthander breezed home with an easy, 4–1 victory. The Orioles had drawn first blood, and as one veteran Baltimore reporter put it, "The Mets needed this first one to prove to everyone that they were a team of destiny," he said. "Instead, the Orioles showed them who the boss is. . . . I wouldn't be surprised if Baltimore walks away with it in four or five games."

A pair of lefthanders, Koosman and McNally, started the second game and matched goose eggs for three innings. In the fourth the Mets drew first blood when Donn Clendenon belted a solo homer over the left-center-field fence. It stayed that way through six. Not only was Jerry Koosman shutting the Orioles out, he also hadn't given up a single hit.

But then Paul Blair opened the seventh with a single, stole second, and came home on a base hit by Brooks Robinson. The game was tied. If the Orioles could pull it out, they would have a tremendous advantage with a two-game lead. But going into the ninth inning, the game was still tied at 1–1.

McNally retired the first two Mets in the ninth, but then a pair of singles by Charles and Grote put two runners on base. Normally weak-hitting Al Weis surprised everyone by stroking a single to right to drive home the go-ahead run. The Mets were now three outs away from tying the series.

Like McNally, Koosman retired the first two, but then walked Frank Robinson and Powell. Manager Hodges then brought Ron Taylor in to face Brooks Robinson, and the veteran righty got Robinson on a bouncer out to third. The Mets won the game 2–1, had tied the series, and were now coming home to New York for the next three games. Perhaps the momentum had shifted.

It was rookie Gentry against Jim Palmer in game three. And this time it was the Mets who got off first. Tommie Agee led off the bottom of the first with a long home run, and an inning later pitcher Gentry doubled to drive in two more, giving the New Yorkers an early, 3–0 advantage. Then, in the fourth inning, the Mets began performing miracles once more.

The Orioles had two men on with two out when catcher Ellie Hendricks stroked a long drive into the gap in left-center-field. It looked like a "'tweener" that would roll to the wall and score at least two runs. But Tommie Agee, who was shaded to right, began running full speed toward the descending baseball.

At the last second, Agee lunged across his body with his gloved hand and grabbed the ball just as it was falling past him. The ball caught in the very tip of the webbing of his glove, looking like an ice cream cone. But he held on, and it was not only one of the great catches in World Series history, but it also prevented a pair of runs from crossing the plate.

In the sixth, the Mets got another run to increase

New York Mets centerfielder Tommie Agee makes a diving catch of a Paul Blair drive with the bases loaded in the seventh inning of game three of the 1969 World Series. Agee's catch saved the game and the Mets went on to win the series in five games, one of the great upsets in series history. (AP/Wide World Photo)

their lead to 4–0. But in the seventh, the Orioles loaded the bases against the tiring Gary Gentry. With Paul Blair due up, manager Hodges removed Gentry in favor of hard-throwing Nolan Ryan. Not wanting to walk in a run, the sometimes wild Ryan pitched carefully. He took something off his fastball and Blair tagged it.

The ball rocketed out toward right center. Once again it looked like a sure extra-base hit, one that would score three runs. But suddenly there was Agee again, running full tilt toward the sinking baseball. This time the centerfielder dove headfirst, extending his glove as far as he could, and he caught the ball just before it hit the ground. He rolled over twice, but then thrust his glove in the air with the ball still inside it.

Seeing that Agee had held the ball, the fans at Shea let out a thunderous roar. Agee's second catch was just as spectacular as his first, and more importantly, the two grabs had saved at least five runs from scoring. An Ed Kranepool homer gave the Mets a fifth run in the eighth, and Ryan held the Orioles in check the rest of the way to complete the 5–0 victory, giving the Mets a 2–1 lead in the series. Could the impossible be really happening?

Sensing the growing feeling that the Mets were a team of destiny, veteran Brooks Robinson tried to settle his team down. "The Mets are not supermen," he said. "They're just flesh and blood. Our turn will come tomorrow."

Frank Robinson also promised his team would be back. "There are no bowed heads in here," he said. "And no one is feeling sorry for himself. But the Mets aren't lucky. I respected them before this started and I respect them now. But we're not through."

But the Mets now had their ace, Tom Seaver, ready to go again. And if there was one thing the young Met pitcher wanted, it was to win a World Series game. He looked at the game as the most important of his life. And once again he would be facing the crafty Mike Cuellar.

Seaver got a quick boost this time. Donn Clendenon belted a second-inning homer to put the New Yorkers on the scoreboard. Both pitchers had their good stuff and the slim lead held up right into the ninth inning. Now Seaver took the mound again, knowing that he was three outs away from winning the ballgame and giving his team a commanding, 3–1, series lead.

With one out, however, Frank Robinson singled and Boog Powell followed with another base hit, putting runners on first and third with the dangerous Brooks Robinson coming up. Seaver worked carefully, but Robinson picked out a low fastball and drilled it sharply into the right-center-field gap. If it fell in, the Orioles would surely take the lead.

Everyone looked for Agee once again. But this time the centerfielder was just too far away. But suddenly, there was rightfielder Ron Swoboda, charging headlong toward the ball. With Mets fans praying for one more incredible catch, Swoboda dove for the baseball. If he missed, it could roll to the wall for an inside-the-park home run. But just before he hit the ground, Swoboda stretched his left arm out in front of him and caught the ball a split second before it hit the turf.

115

Frank Robinson alertly tagged at third and came home to score the tying run. But Swoboda's catch had prevented more damage. Seaver got out of the inning, but the game was tied. The Mets didn't score in their half of the ninth, and when the Orioles failed to score in the top of the tenth, Seaver saw his chance to win slipping away.

"I knew Gil [Hodges] wouldn't let me go any further," he said. "I was just hoping we could push something across in our half of the inning."

It didn't take the Mets long to get started. When leftfielder Don Buford lost Jerry Grote's fly in the sun, it fell untouched for a double. Rod Gaspar went in to pinch-run for Grote and reliever Dick Hall then walked Al Weis to put runners on first and second with none out. Reserve catcher J. C. Martin then pinch-hit for Seaver and bunted. Reliever Pete Richert, who had just come into the game, fielded the bunt and threw toward first. But the ball hit Martin in the arm and bounced away. As it did, Rod Gaspar, who had rounded third, just kept coming home, scoring the winning run!

"When I saw Rodney running home," Seaver said later, "I just watched those last ten steps. And when he hit the plate, I said to myself, 'My God, I've won a World Series game. I've won!'"

The Orioles tried to claim that Martin was out of the baseline when the ball hit him, but to no avail. The run counted and the Mets had won, giving them a 3–1 lead in the series. Besides the great catches and freak plays, their pitchers had been doing their job. Baltimore scored just six runs in the first four games. They couldn't win with offensive production like that. Now, in game five, it was Koosman against McNally once again.

This time the Orioles drew first blood. Only it wasn't one of their vaunted sluggers who got the job done. Instead, it was pitcher McNally, who surprised everyone by belting a two-run homer off Koosman to give his club the lead in the third inning. And later in the same frame Frank Robinson slammed a solo shot to up the lead to 3–0. The two homers marked the first Orioles extra-base hits since early in the first game.

But then Koosman settled down and held the Orioles in check into the sixth inning. The problem was the Mets hadn't been able to dent McNally as yet. Then in the bottom of the sixth Cleon Jones reached first when Manager Hodges proved he was hit by a pitch by showing the umpire a smudge of shoe polish on the baseball. More Mets magic?

Whether the incident unnerved McNally or not is hard to say, but the next batter, Donn Clendenon, promptly slammed his third homer of the series and put the Mets back in the ballgame at 3–2. An inning later, little Al Weis, a singles hitter at best, shocked everyone by putting a McNally pitch over the left-field wall. Weis's home tied the game at 3–3, and the huge crowd at Shea Stadium began to get the feeling that their team was about to make history.

Koosman continued to mow down the Orioles, and then in the bottom of the eighth, Cleon Jones opened up with a double. With one out, Swoboda slammed a double down the right-field line, scoring Jones with the go-ahead run. With two out, first baseman Powell bobbled Jerry Grote's ground ball and then threw late to first as still another run crossed the plate. The Mets now led 5–3, and the Orioles were down to their last three outs.

Once again Koosman went to work. After Frank Robinson led off with a walk, he induced Powell to hit into a fielder's choice. Brooks Robinson flied to right for the second out. Up came Davey Johnson, the Orioles' second baseman, and ironically, a man who would later manage the New York Mets to another world championship in 1986.

But this time all Johnson could do was lift a lazy fly to left field. Cleon Jones camped under it, knelt down on one knee, and let the ball settle into his glove. He stayed frozen in that position for a few more seconds until everyone realized what had just happened. Then pandemonium broke out everywhere.

The New York Mets had become champions of the baseball world, rising from the depth of tenth place two years before and ninth place a year earlier to win it all. And they had done it with great pitching, timely hitting, and a few minor miracles in the field to beat a team considered the best in baseball by far. It had to be one of the greatest upsets in sports history.

Just a few short years earlier, Casey Stengel had looked around at his Mets and asked if anyone there could play the game. Now the answer was a resounding YES! As veteran third baseman Ed Charles put it:

"We're number one in the world and you just can't get any bigger than that."